Bob Moats

I0567068

AREA 51 MURDERS

By Bob Moats

Area 51 Murders

ISBN – 978-0-9903138-4-7

For information and address:
Magic 1 Productions
P.O. Box 524, Fraser MI 48026-0524
Website: http://murdernovels.com
Cover by Bob Moats

Other Jim Richards series books by Bob Moats

(In Series Order)
Classmate Murders
Vegas Showgirl Murders
Dominatrix Murders
Mistress Murders
Bridezilla Murders
Magic Murders
Strip Club Murders
Made-for-TV Murders
Mystery Cruise Murders
Talk Show Murders
Sin City Murders
Black Widow Murders
Vegas Vigilante Murders
Area 51 Murders
Mortuary Murders
Hypnotic Murders
Sunshine State Murders
Blue Suede Murders
Honky Tonk Murders
Dark Carnival Murders
Lipstick Murders
Pasta Murders
Talent Show Murders
Shyster Murders
Campground Murders
Network Murders
Reunion Murders
Big Apple Murders
Kennel Murders
Trick or Treat Murders
Santa Murders
Wiseguy Murders

For a preview or to purchase a book, go to
http://murdernovels.com

What a few people are saying about Murder Novels by Bob Moats

"I went online this morning and read your book. I thought at first that I would only read a few pages, but got sucked into it and read 11 chapters. You are a very good writer! I read quite a bit and often pick up "Airport" paperback mysteries to read on a plane. Most of them are dreadful, with obvious plots. Classmate Murders is a much better story than most."

Ray Zink.

"I got up to chapter ten of the Classmate Murders and decided then to buy the next two books." ... "Just finished your third book, the Dominatrix Murders. I thought it was the best one of the three, didn't want to put it down till I finished it. I looked forward to see how Penny would greet (Jim) every day after her show. Keep the books coming can't wait for the next one."

A. Norris.

"If you like mysteries and action then don't miss reading this book..."

Jan Schneider.

"I haven't finished the book yet, when I enjoy a book, I take my time, but I want to buy the other two books. I compare your writing to a Mickey Spillane novel, and I like your style, very narrative. I'm amazed you don't have a publisher yet."
Michael Rasah, Professor of History.

"Thanks for making me immortal, love the stories, your friend, Buck."
The real "Buck", George Carver

Extra special thanks to:

Special thanks to Val Brooks who edited this book, for her great suggestions and sharing the stories about her father that became the basis for the character Major Colin Rickson.

Thank you to all the people who purchased this book. I hope you enjoy it as much as I enjoyed writing it for my faithful readers.

The Jim Richards Family of Readers is listed in the back of the book.

Area 51 Murders
By Bob Moats

Chapter 1

The razor wire was meant to cut into the skin of any person trying to escape over the fence. It was doing its job on Darryl's arms, body and legs as he tried to go over the fence to get out from the U.S. military's base 85 miles north of Las Vegas, the infamous Area 51.

Darryl didn't care so much that his body was being shredded by the sharp coils of metal atop the fence; he just wanted to escape from the insanity of what he had witnessed in the restricted area that the government denied existed. He was now being followed by forces, ones who wanted him to stay in the compound, and to be a guinea pig for their experiments. Not something he wanted to be subjected to.

He fell to the ground on the free side of the fence; but was suddenly surrounded by military personnel, holding their high-powered rifles and handguns on him. He laid there frustrated by the men who had no thoughts of what he went through in the secret base, which very few people on earth had any concept of what was actually going on there. He just laid back and let them take him. Screw it, he thought, he now didn't care.

Bob Moats

~~*~~

Richards Investigations was gaining a little notoriety from its involvement in the Vigilante murders case. The police commissioner had given me his thanks publicly for my aid in finding the killer, so now I was being sought out to solve all kinds of cases. I didn't mind it, but at sixty-two years, I didn't want to become overworked now. I actually enjoyed the slow pace days back before the press made a big deal out of it. I had enough money in the bank from my book sales and I really didn't need to work hard if I didn't want to. Being a private eye was fun for me, but now it was becoming work.

My beautiful and sometimes odd wife Penny slapped my butt, telling me to get my ass out of bed. I pulled the pillow over my head and tried to ignore her, but she's not one you can ignore. She grabbed on the sheets and gave a good pull, exposing me to the harsh reality of Sunday morning. She left our bedroom and went off into the house to plot her day, followed by Willy, our toy Yorkie.

I pulled myself up and forced myself to the shower where I put on the cold water by mistake and nearly froze my still sleeping body, a definite eye-opener. I toweled off and throwing on a robe, went to the kitchen. Penny was eating her usual morning bowl of oatmeal as I put my two pieces of bread in the toaster.

"What wondrous things are we going to do today?" she asked between spoonfuls of mush.

"I haven't given it a thought," I said as I was trying to coax the toaster to accept the bread, it just kept popping up before it toasted the slices. "Between the two of us, we have enough money to buy a new toaster. You love shopping let's go buy one," I said before realizing what came out of my mouth.

Her eyes lit up on that thought, she finished the last bite of her oatmeal and said, "I'll get ready, the mall is calling." She went off as I regretted initiating a shopping trip. I didn't mind shopping now that I had money to buy silly things, but shopping with Penny was work for me.

The house phone rang and I hoped it would spare me from a trip to the mall. "Hello?" I said.

It was Lacey, my office manager-slash-receptionist. She had recently married Mac, the supervisor for my friend and partner Buck's security guard business. The two of them took in and adopted Jessie, the nine-year-old whose abusive father was murdered by the vigilante and then Penny and I had her for a couple weeks before she went with Lacey and Mac.

"I hope you are calling to say there's a big case needing my attention," I said hopefully.

"Why, does Penny have something for you to do?"

"Shopping," I said.

"Oh, well I could make something up to get you out of it."

"No, that all right. What's up?"

"Mac and I are having a backyard barbeque next weekend and wanted to invite you and Penny."

"I'm sure we can make it. How's married life?"

"We're doing well and Jessie is a joy to have with us. Mac is starting to spoil her; I have to be the bad guy when they start plotting."

"Enjoy every minute of it. My son grew up so fast it was as if it never happened. I'll tell Penny about your BBQ and I'll see you at the office tomorrow morning."

"I'll be there after I get Jessie off to school," She said as we finished our call.

Penny came back in and asked who was on the phone, I thought about telling her it was a case needing my immediate attention, but she always knew when I was fibbing. She had this telepathy that I couldn't avoid, maybe she's an alien from outer space.

"It was Lacey; we're invited to a BBQ next weekend at their home."

"Good, we can see Jessie again. So shall we go attack the mall?"

I was grinning but feeling dread. "Sure, off to buy a new toaster."

We went to the garage to get my car and headed to the huge mall a couple miles from our home on the far western edge of Las Vegas. The view from our house of the Vegas valley and the tall buildings of the Vegas strip, made our home worth living in. We attacked the mall, or I should say Penny attacked the mall; I just kept up with her. We found a big toaster in Macy's that I was sure could make the bread, toast and butter it all at one time, so we bought it. I was fulfilled, but Penny was still raring to go.

Half of our shopping time was usually spent with Penny being recognized for her morning TV talk show and having to stop and talk to her fans. No one recognized me; I was just Penny's husband. After about three hours of shopping and lunch in the food court, we headed back home.

We spent the rest of the day relaxing; Penny swam in the pool most of the day while I was in my home office typing on the keyboard trying to finish my third book about the Dominatrix murders back in Michigan. Willy was lounging by the pool, I guess he had enough of swimming by himself, and I think he missed Jessie.

Buck called me to say he picked up another car dealership for his guards. He mentioned about a body found up by Area 51, everyone was saying he was murdered by aliens.

"Buck, there would be no body if aliens killed the guy, they would disintegrate him with their death rays, leaving only a dust pile," I said.

"Well, the people up there say they saw strange lights and heard loud noises coming from where the body was dumped. That's how they found him; they followed the lights. I tell you it was little green men."

"Why are they always little green men, why not chartreuse, an off green color that would give them a little fashion sense. And why little, are they munchkins from over the rainbow?"

"Now you're being silly. They're not munchkins; they're from outer space, not Oz."

"Maybe so, but I'm not going to worry about it. Are you going to be in the office tomorrow?"

"I'll be there early to get the paperwork ready for the new job. I'll probably be there when you get in."

"Okay, see you in the morning, and don't get abducted by little green men."

"Now you're making fun of it. I do believe in them."

"I do too; I just don't think they would murder someone and dump the body."

"Okay you have a point. See you tomorrow," He said and hung up.

I looked out my window and saw Penny was sunbathing by the pool now on her stomach, her bikini top was off and she was looking at me looking at her. I waved and she flashed me her naked breasts and then dropped back down, laughing. For a fifty-nine year-old woman she still had a great body and was still beautiful. Her youthful look helped for her talk show, which was doing well in the ratings since she started here. I did miss the days back in Michigan when she would bring odd things home from her talk show there, and drive me crazy with them. My best memory was when she was made up to look like Marilyn Monroe by the drag queens she had on her show, I got to take Marilyn to bed with me. It was nice.

I went back to my story just as my cell phone rang, the caller ID said it was Deacon.

"Hey big guy, what's up?" I said.

"You read a lot of books don't you?" he said.

"Yes, I have read a good number, why?"

"You ever read science fiction stories?"

"Sure, Ray Bradbury was my favorite author along with H. G. Wells. Again, why?"

"Did you read the Sunday Review-Journal this morning?" He asked as I remembered that I forgot to pick-up the paper.

"No, is there some big crime in it that needs my attention."

"Well, there was a murder out by Area 51 that may need looking into. I got a call from some woman who was married to the victim, she called me because the newspapers said that I knew you, she was looking for you to find her husband's killer."

**

Chapter 2

"She could have called my office," I said.

"She did, but got your answering machine. You aren't listed in the book for your personal numbers and she read in the papers that we worked together on the vigilante case. She called Metro and they got hold of me, I told her to go to your office in the morning and I gave her the directions."

"Buck said it was little green men who killed the guy."

"Little green men wouldn't murder someone and just dump the body," Deacon said smiling through the phone.

"That's just what I said! So this woman is wife to the murdered victim. Why doesn't she let the police handle it?"

"The guy was murdered on federal property, the locals can't touch it and don't want to. The Feds are not moving on it fast enough or so the wife says. She wants her own investigation into it, ergo you."

"Ergo? Are you learning new words now?"

"Lynn bought me one of those word-a-day books, to improve my vocabulary. I guess I'm not refined enough."

"I like you just the way you are, don't go changing a hair on your head."

Area 51 Murders

He laughed and said, "I'll call you later tomorrow to see how it went. Paranormal cases make good books, maybe there's one in this for you."

"True, but its vampires and werewolves that are what's selling now. Maybe he was killed by a vampire."

"Whatever, call me," he said and finished the call.

I looked out to Penny again and she was not in her spot. I turned my head to see her coming in my door, still missing her bikini top.

"You look delicious, what do you have on your mind?"

"Come with me to the bedroom and I'll show you," she said with her evil little smile.

She got no arguments from me.

We came out of the bedroom about an hour later and sat on our favorite place, the couch. I remoted the TV and found a comedy that we watched. During a commercial, I got up to go to the kitchen and nuke a couple of pocket sandwiches and we ate them washing them down with beer.

I told her about Deacon's call. "I hope I get to chase aliens now."

"The only aliens you can chase around here are from south of the border. They aren't green either. I had an alien chaser and a person who claims they were abducted by aliens on my show back in Michigan. I'll fill you in on what I learned later."

"It may help, but I don't think this has anything to do with little green men. So I'm not going to be looking for outer space aliens."

"You are an outer space alien," she said and kissed me on the nose.

~~*~~

I was into my office early the next morning; Lacey was at her desk typing something. She smiled and said good morning. I went to the counter, "I'm expecting a woman coming in this morning to hire me to find her husband's killer. Let me know as soon as she comes in."

"Is this about the aliens?" she said.

I stood just amazed how everyone is one-step ahead of me, "Yes it is; how did you know?

"Buck came in babbling about aliens and some guy who was murdered out in Area 51. I just put that together with your case."

"I may have to start taking you out on cases with me," I said with a smile.

"I'd love that, oh and Trapper wanted to see you as soon as you came in."

Area 51 Murders

"Thanks," I said and went back to his office. He was sitting back in his chair staring at the ceiling. "Don't strain yourself thinking too hard."

He almost fell back in his chair when I said that. He straightened up and asked me to sit. I did.

"I got a call from my lady friend Sam, she has a problem with her brother, he's missing. She asked me if I could find him, so I'll be out for a few days hunting him down. That's not going to mess up any plans you may have."

"Nope, I have nothing but a possible case coming in this morning. A guy was murdered out by Area 51 and his wife is looking for me to find his killer. Now I'm going to try and avoid all the little green men jokes."

"Well, it's a big deal out here; Area 51 attracts tons of strange types who all want to see the Grand Poobah of Pluto. And the towns around Groom Lake, where Area 51 is, all cater to those nut jobs."

"I don' think this guy has anything to do with aliens, I'm sure that we'll find out it was a terrestrial creature who did the deed. What do you know about Area 51?"

"Officially, the name Area 51 was dropped by the government in the 70's, but movies and television kept the name alive. The place was originally a base for testing spy planes and other top-secret aircraft such as Lockheed U-2, the SR-71 Blackbird, the F-117 stealth fighter, Northrop's B-2 stealth bomber, the mysterious Aurora Project, and possibly even alien spacecraft. Or so I hear, but I'm not into aliens. The base is not actually fenced, but the entire boundary of the base is patrolled by a private security service, backed by the Lincoln County Sheriffs, equipped with high-tech surveillance gear and a network of sensors that can detect anyone moving on the property. Try to get on the property and get yourself detained by very angry men."

"You sound like a tour guide," I said smiling.

"Back when I was in high school in Vegas, I had a part-time job giving informational speeches for the helicopter tours. I kept the tourists in line happy before they got on the whirly-birds."

"And you remember this all these years later?"

"Hey, when you repeat the same lines over and over hundreds of times a day, you don't forget." He laughed as I heard the bell on the front door tinkle.

"That may be my client now," I said and I went towards the front. I came to the lobby and saw a woman, rather short, plain, dishwater blonde hair, about thirtyish standing at the counter. Lacey smiled to me as I came out.

"Jim, this is Mrs. Huston, she's here to see you."

"Thank you, Lacey. Mrs. Huston, please come to my office." I showed her the way and we went in, I asked her to sit. "Are you the person who called my friend Detective DeAngelo to locate me?" I asked.

"Yes, I had read in the newspapers about the vigilante murders and how you helped find him. I called here but got your answering machine, I had to talk to you as soon as possible before the government buries my husband's case without finding his killer. I know they will sweep it under the rug."

"Just what happened that you know of?"

"I was told my husband, Mark, was found dead on the property the government maintains at Groom Lake installation known as Area 51. The local police can't investigate because it's federal property. The sheriff was apologetic and said his hands were tied because the Air Force took charge of the murder. I'm getting no help from the government people, they say they are investigating and would keep me informed but they won't."

"Why do you say that?"

"They have been very abrupt with me, not friendly at all, and not very open to releasing my husband so I can get an autopsy. They say they are taking care of it. Since it happened the other day, I have heard nothing but excuses. I need someone outside of the system, so I came to you."

"Well, I appreciate the vote of confidence; I'll try and see what I can do to help you." I handed her the pad and pencil and continued, "Write down any names of people you have talked to about this so I can contact them to get my investigation started."

She took a couple minutes writing on the pad and handed it back to me. It had three names, all Air Force people.

"OK, I'll see what I can do for you. Do you live near Groom Lake?"

"Yes, we have a home in Rachel, Nevada, northeast of Groom Lake. Mark would drive everyday almost fifty miles to go to work there. He worked for a private contractor working on the new hangers on the base. He came home last week and said he found out a way to make lots of money, but couldn't say what it was. I was worried he'd try another of his harebrained ideas to make a quick buck. I think it's what got him killed. He probably stuck his nose in where he shouldn't have."

I handed the pad and pencil back and asked her to write down the name of the company he worked for, she did.

"I don't have much money, with Mark working on the base, he was the income maker. I can't work due to a spinal problem I have. I'll try and make payments if that's acceptable."

"No, it's not acceptable. I'm not going to charge you for this; it's the least I can do to find your husband's killer. Besides, I love harassing the government. Is that acceptable to you?"

"Thank you, Mr. Richards. I'm really lost without my Mark. We've been married for twelve good years; it's going to be hard on me and our son."

"How old is your son?"

"He's just eleven, I haven't told him about his father yet, I don't know how to get myself up to doing it."

She started to tear up and I handed her a tissue from my emergency box by the desk. I was trying not to tear up myself thinking about the boy losing his father. I was now determined that I would find the murderer.

**

Chapter 3

"You drove a long ways to get here; I'll do what I can to help you. Where is your son now?"

"He's with my mother, in Rachel. I had to take a bus here, the base has Mark's car and they aren't going to release it yet."

"This is ridiculous, no way for the government to treat its citizens. Wait here," I said and went out of my office to Buck's office.

He was sitting at his desk working on some papers. "Hey guy, you have an extra guard doing nothing?"

"Sure, what do you need watched?"

"Nothing, I need a taxi service. I have a woman in my office who needs a ride back to her home up by Area 51," I said to make him perk up, he did.

"Damn, is this the wife of the guy killed by aliens?"

"Yes, she's the wife and no, he wasn't killed by aliens. Let's get over that. Now can I get someone to take her home? She came all the way down here by bus and I can't see making her go back that way."

"That's about ninety miles one way, three hour trip up and back, I'll be happy to take her myself. I can get to see the places where they cater to alien chasers. I love it."

"Whatever, I appreciate it. Come meet her." I went back to my office, Buck came shortly after and I introduced them.

"Pleasure to meet you ma'am." Buck spoke softly. She smiled up to the big man and shook his hand. Buck turned to me and asked, "Are you taking the case?"

"Yes I am."

"Well, I'd like to be part of it, two heads are always better than one." He gave us his walrus smile.

"That works for me." I turned to Mrs. Huston and said, "Buck is going to drive you home, you shouldn't have to take a bus. Buck may drive you crazy about the aliens in Area 51, just put up with him," I said with a smile.

She laughed and said, "I have some tales to tell him on the way. He may go crazy listening to me."

Buck said, "That's great, shall we go?"

"I have everything I need, for now, we may come to visit you in Rachel, so Buck will get the address and after I make some calls, I'll let you know what to expect."

"Thank you, Mr. Richards. I'll be waiting to hear from you."

Buck escorted the woman to one of the new cars we had for the guard service and they went off. I went to Trapper's office and sat.

"How do I get information about Area 51, and its secrets?" I asked.

"Try Google, you always do."

"I want more detail than that, I need to find out the dirty secrets."

"Why don't you call our buddy Earl Daws back in Michigan, he's got the inside on the dirty secrets when it comes to the government."

"Yeah, that's good; I can ask if he is treating our branch office out there with care. I wonder if Paula is still with him."

"Call and find out."

"I will," I said and went back to my office and picked up the phone. I called Earl.

"It took you long enough to call, I thought you forgot about us back here," Earl said when I identified myself.

"I didn't forget you, much. How's my office doing out there?"

"It's still standing. I redecorated the interior though, it early dark crime noir, lots of blacks and posters from old crime movies. Bogey looks good as Sam Spade. I'll send you some photos."

"Thanks, is Paula still around?"

"My foxy redhead, she sure is. She's out right now getting us some coffee and donuts."

"I hope you aren't using petty cash."

"Nope, I have money. So, what's up?"

"You have been around the block a few times, what do you know about Area 51?"

"I know enough to stay away from it. The government takes their national security seriously. But I have been on the base in the past; I had to fly out with one of their spy planes on a mission to Columbia, but that's not for publication. They drove us onto the base in a mini-van with blocked out windows, drove us up to the plane and took us straight to the thing after warning us not to dawdle and no looking around. I thought Black Ops was tough; these Area 51 troops are dangerous. Does that scare you enough to stay away from the place?"

"Hell no, you know me, I like a challenge."

"Well, seriously, be careful. Those people don't fool around and they turn you over to Homeland Security who don't need a reason to lock you away. I can't bail you out there; I've called in just about all my markers to help you."

Area 51 Murders

I could hear him stifle a laugh; I knew he could blackmail and whatever else he needed to get people to help him.

"I have a murder case of a worker on the base and his wife says the government people aren't being very cooperative. His name is Mark Huston if you get a chance to waste a phone call for me."

"Oh, I may have a little time between chasing cheating spouses to check on it for you. I may have a marker or two left."

"Great, I appreciate it."

"How's my other girlfriend doing?"

"Penny? She got a new talk show out here called Vegas Alive and she's happy with it. Buck has started a security guard service for us and it's doing well. We now have almost a hundred employees; I'm glad Buck takes care of the paperwork."

"Can't keep Penny away from the camera can you? She looks good for it; I hope you don't give her worry lines now if you go chasing aliens."

"Don't start with the aliens, I got Buck all fired up on them. See what you can find out and keep in touch."

"Yeah, well don't take another two months to call; I need to know what's going on out there before I decide to move in with you. Do you have enough work to keep an old Black Ops agent busy?"

"Old is the operative word, yes the office is getting busy now with the cases we've had recently. I may need another body out here. I let you know."

"Great, I'll check on your dead guy and get back with you." He disconnected and I sat back thinking about my attack on the secret base that everyone knew about.

Buck came back three and a half hours later with a big smile on his face, wearing a ball cap that had "I was abducted in Area 51" printed on it. He handed me his digital camera and turned on the preview to show me all the sights he saw along the road to Area 51. Most of them were restaurants and tourist traps to sell alien stuff.

"I hope you didn't buy anything else, like genuine alien poop."

"Hey, do I look like a tourist? No, I got genuine pictures of alien saucers hovering over the base. They even have a certificate of authenticity by the man who took the pictures." He was grinning widely and I didn't want to spoil his fun.

"Fine, how did your trip with Mrs. Huston go?"

"We had a real nice ride. She told me stories that her husband told her about the base and the work he was doing there. It should help with our investigation."

Our investigation? Well, if Buck wanted to come along for the ride I was happy with it. He could investigate as well as I could. As he said, two heads are better than one. Besides, he had this thing for Area 51, so he'd be more apt to want to go in to look it over. He wasn't bothered by danger.

"So what's our attack on this?" Buck asked.

"Well, I called Earl back in Michigan and he's going to see what he can find about Mark Huston. We need to go talk to Mark's employer to see what his job entailed and what they may know. Then we investigate." I said with a smile.

"Works for me. On the way up to the quaint little town of Rachel, I'll fill you in on what Mrs. Huston told me about Mark's harebrain ideas to make money and that he had something in mind involving Area 51."

"Good, all we can do now is wait to see if Earl can get us something. It's late so let's call it a day."

"What's Trapper up to?"

"He left a couple hours ago to track down the missing brother of his lady friend, Sam."

"The bookie woman you found during the Black Widow murders?"

"Yep, Trapper has a thing for her. I think she's his first girlfriend he's had since he lived here years ago. The girlfriend who died in an auto accident, one of the reasons he doesn't say good-bye to people. He needed some healing for that and I think Sam fills that need."

"Yeah, I noticed he's been a lot nicer lately. Let's encourage that romance."

Chapter 4

Penny was all excited about my investigating Area 51. "Can I go too?" she asked.

"I don't think so," I said as I packed a small suitcase with enough clothes to last a few days. I hoped it would only be a few days. "It may not be the safest place for even Buck and me, so I don't want to subject you to another kidnapping. How many has it been now, three?"

"I've lost count, I should write a book on how to handle being kidnapped. Well, if I can't go, then take lots of pictures."

"I will. Did I tell you Trapper is going on a case to find the missing brother of his new lady love?"

"No, why is he missing and where is he?"

"If I knew that, Trapper wouldn't be looking for him, now would he?"

"Oh, right. So, are you going to keep a record of your trip so I can enjoy it?"

"I'll give you all the gory details and maybe I'll see about bringing back an alien for you."

"As long as he is handsome and viral."

"Maybe I'll bring back a female alien."

"You do, then don't come back."

Area 51 Murders

I kissed her on the lips with tongue, so she'd shut up. "I'll call you every day, if you don't hear from me, I've been abducted."

"I'm not paying the ransom."

"I love you too," I said as I closed the suitcase and went out of the bedroom, followed by Penny and Willy. I put my suitcase by the front door and went to the kitchen to get a couple cold beers, one for Penny and one for me. My adorable wife was already sitting on the couch with the TV on. She found a good crime show so we relaxed and watched it enjoying our beer and chips. We were so comfortable together, I was happy that I had found her back when we were chasing the classmate killers. All the years from when we graduated, I didn't know she harbored a crush for me from high school.

Around eight, my cell phone rang, caller ID said it was Earl. I went to the kitchen to take the call. "Isn't it past your bed time out there?" I asked.

"It's only eleven; I'm just getting warmed up. I have a little info on your Huston guy, everyone is very tight lipped about it. I called Harold Kettering again; he's still enjoying the memories from our cruise ship trip to Tahiti. He called a few people he knew, and is getting not much info, but he says that Huston was found just outside the base proper. He was still on the grid for Area 51 but more on the Nellis Air Force Range property. No one seems to know what the other is doing about it, so the body is being shuffled back and forth between the Nellis Air Force and the Area 51 command. Harold said they might release the body to the wife this week, after they do an internal investigation. I doubt they will have anything conclusive to offer, just a lot of double talk. I will say this, Huston wasn't murdered by aliens." I heard him stifle a laugh.

"That's my opinion, even if Buck says otherwise. Thanks for that much. Now what should I do to proceed with my investigation?"

"Keep your head low and cover your ass," he said with a loud laugh. "Otherwise, be nice to the Lincoln County Sheriffs, they may help you with it. Harold said you could throw his name around if it helps."

"Great, I'm heading up to Rachel, Nevada in the morning to see the wife again. I'll see if she knows anyone in the sheriff's department who can help."

"Works for me, be careful and talk later." He disconnected and I sat thinking. Unfortunately, there was nothing to think on, this case would have to proceed step by step, no plotting here for unknown facts.

I went to my computer, brought up the Las Vegas Review-Journal online newspaper, and dug around until I found the article on the death in Area 51. The story told very little, just names and places of the people involved. They stated that due to security, they couldn't get much more information about the murder. It was more of a fluff piece for the paper, using the Area 51 name. I shut it down, went back to the couch and told Penny what little I knew, then we finished up watching television and went to bed.

Early next morning, Penny was rushing around getting ready to go interview her guests and she was taking Willy with her to the studio. I called Lacey to tell her not to pick up the dog and asked if Buck had gotten there yet. She said he had, I told her to tell him I'd be there soon and hung up.

Penny came into the living room to gather her things and said, "I called Lacey earlier and asked if Jessie could come visit with me over the weekend while you're gone, we girls need to shop," she said with an evil grin.

"Fine, just don't spoil her, Aunty Penny. I'll call you with my progress." I kissed her and she went off. I gathered everything I thought I would need for the trip and the investigation, all my spy gadgets and personal things and went out to the car.

The ride to my office was not bad, little traffic today, which was unusual for morning rush hour. I got to the office and parked in the back waving to our guard at the gate of the secured parking lot. We put the guard on the gate when the owner of the building said he couldn't keep anyone on the job. Since our office is right there, we would protect the lot and the employees of the other businesses in the strip mall. Plus we got a small cut in the rent.

I went in and straight to Buck's office after checking in on Trapper, who wasn't in his office. I presumed he was out chasing errant brothers. Buck was talking to Mac, and they finished when I arrived at the door.

"Morning Mac," I said. He said morning back and then stood.

"Are you and Penny coming to our BBQ this weekend?" he asked.

"Well, Penny will be there, she's having Jessie over to our place for the weekend since I'm going to be away with Buck chasing a killer. Didn't Buck mention it?" I said as I looked to Buck.

"No he didn't," Mac said also looking to Buck.

"Well, it slipped my mind," Buck defended.

"We're going hunting aliens and it slipped your mind?" I said.

"Yes it slipped my mind, I had a lot of things to think about."

"You said you were going to be gone this week, and that's why you wanted me to watch the guards, you didn't say you were going ghost hunting." Mac said.

"Alien hunting, no ghosts, at least I hope there are no ghosts," Buck replied.

"Whatever, I hope you can make it another weekend," Mac said to me.

"I'm sure we will, thanks." Mac went out and I sat in the chair he vacated.

"So are you ready to go?"

"Yep, I got all my gear in the car already," he said.

Area 51 Murders

"We're not taking one of the Vibes are we?"

"Oh hell, no. Trapper was nice enough to let us use his Jeep Cherokee; he took the Vibe. The jeep will be better for desert exploring and alien chasing."

"I'm surprised Trapper let you borrow the car, knowing the times he had chased you in his cop car ten miles through Macomb County and three mall parking lots."

"You're not going to let that drop, that was years ago."

"Hey, if I want a good wheel man you are the one. Shall we go?" I stood and went to the lobby and up to the counter. I stood watching Lacey working on the computer until she saw me and jumped.

"I'm going to put a bell around you; you keep sneaking up and scaring me."

"Well, you are too wrapped up in your own little world to be aware of what is going on around you."

"So is Penny going to pick up Jessie after school?" she said changing the subject.

"Yep, be aware that they are going shopping so make some space in Jessie's room." Buck came up behind me and said he was ready. "Okay Lacey hold down the fort, see you in a couple days, hopefully." She said her good-byes to Buck and me, and then we went out the back lot to Trapper's Jeep.

Buck was in his glory behind the wheel. We drove out highway 15 then over to 93 up to Crystal Springs where we caught the 357 right into Rachel. Along the way, we talked about what we could do once we got there. I said, "We needed to talk to his employers who had the contract for work on the base, to see what Huston was doing. We can go into visit the Lincoln County Sheriffs and see if they might have any info to help. Otherwise, we just wing it, and try not to get arrested when we invade Area 51. I'm sure they won't welcome us with open arms."

"Shall we stop and get some tin foil?" Buck asked.

"What on earth for?"

"So we can make hats to prevent the aliens from probing our brains," he grinned.

"Tin foil won't do you any good; you need brains for it to work." I smiled looking out at the scenery.

**

Chapter 5

We drove through excruciatingly boring flat lands on the 357 to Rachel. The mountains in the background loomed large and remote. I think we could drive for days before we reached the mountains, but we weren't going there.

We came up on a rise in the road and then saw it, Rachel. Buck had gotten a bit of info from Louise Huston, the widow, as they drove to the town. He said the town at one time had a good number of people who worked in the Union Carbide mines. But the mines closed and the town slowly lost citizens, now the population hovered around 100 people. Most of the town was mobile homes on pads around the desert area; most pads are now empty. A few trailers still stood for those people who hung in.

Entering the town, we passed a Quik Pik gas station and mini-mart, but it was permanently closed now. Buck had stopped back in Ash Springs to top off the gas tank; there were no gas stations for miles around Rachel, the closest was almost sixty miles north. I'd sure hate to have to walk to a gas station out here, you had to be prepared.

Buck pulled into the drive of Louise's modest boxy trailer home on the edge of Rachel. It was worn by the sun and weather, and I'll bet it glowed in the dark. There had been a good number of atomic bomb tests nearby in years past and the area was probably irradiated. We parked and the door to the trailer opened and out walked Louise, followed by her son. She came up to Buck and me while we stretched our bodies from the long trip.

"Mr. Richards, thank you so much for coming. This isn't the most glamorous place in the world, nothing compared to Las Vegas," she said.

Her son was peeking around her and I smiled to him, "Hi, what's your name?"

He shyly came out from behind his mother and said, "Mitch."

"Nice name Mitch. How are you doing today?"

34

"I'm good, are you the detectives who are going to find my daddy's killer?"

I was taken aback by his comment; yesterday Louise had told me she hadn't told him yet.

She saw my concern and said, "I told him about it last night, we were up very late mourning. He was stronger than I thought."

I looked to the boy and said, "Yes, I'm going to do my best to find out what happened."

He didn't smile, but just ran off around the back of the trailer. "He's been hiding in his tree fort his father built for him most the morning. He took it well, but I think he's holding too much back."

"I understand. Can we go in? It's a bit hot out here in the sun."

"I'm sorry, where are my manners. Yes, come in."

We went into the trailer; it wasn't much cooler in there even with the air conditioner running. There was an older woman sitting in a recliner staring at a TV that wasn't on.

"We don't get television reception out here, tapes and DVD's are our entertainment."

I thought I would scream after living here without television. "Can we sit? I need to ask you a number of questions."

She motioned to the chairs and asked us to sit. "Would you like some lemonade?"

"Yes, that would be nice, if you have it already made."

"Oh we drink it by the gallon here, so it's always handy." She went to the kitchen, pulled out a pitcher from the fridge, and poured two glasses for Buck and me. I thanked her when she returned and sat on the couch.

"Mrs. Huston, may I call you Louise?"

"Sure, you can."

"Good you can call me Jim. Now what did your husband do on the base?"

"He was hired to install wiring in the new hangers. He worked with five other men and they went to the base every weekday. He drove himself to the base but just outside the base, they had to park and a shuttle bus would take them in and to the job site. All very hush-hush. Most of the men in town who work there were warned not to talk about it."

"Did your husband ever break that rule and tell you about his job?"

"Well, he did say that he saw a lot of top secret planes and jets there once in a while. A good number of jets have crashed out here over the years. One came down behind the Quik Pic years back. The base sent men and a huge flatbed truck to haul it away. Just missed a few buildings. One time they wouldn't let us near one of the crashes, they had armed guards and kept us back. All very secretive they are, it's almost silly. Like we'd tell anyone."

"Your husband's employer, is he in town?"

"Yes, it's not really a company, just Fred Parnell working out of his garage. He's one of the few men in town who work on the power poles and wires that provide power to the town. We depend on the power company for our needs, we are kind of a corporate town, run by the power company. Many of the old timers like to use their generators to power their homes, they don't want to be under the thumb of the corporation."

"Can you call him to ask if we can talk to him?"

"Well, you can just yell over the fence, he lives next door." She smiled for the first time since we got here.

"Great, is he home now?"

"I think I saw him out back, let's go find out." She stood; Buck and I followed her out and around the trailer to a gate in the short fence. We went to the trailer next to hers, about twenty yards off. I could see a man standing behind the trailer watching us. He came forward and said, "Louise, I don't want to be rude, but if these men are here to find out what happened to Mark, I can't talk about it. I'm sorry but I depend on the base for my livelihood."

"Sir, I'm Jim Richards and this man is my associate Buck Carson. We're investigators and we just want to ask a couple questions, and won't ask you anything that may be secret to the base. May we talk?"

Area 51 Murders

"Ask, but I may not answer if it's the wrong questions."

"Thank you, I'm wondering how Mark was left on the base if your crew had to be together on and off?"

"No offense, Louise, but Mark was always a trouble maker. Not in the bad sense, he loved practical jokes and did some stupid things, but he somehow slipped off the back of the bus after being counted on by the base guards. We drove off thinking he was with us, and didn't even realize he was gone when we got to the cars. He rode in that morning with Harley Musken, so there was no extra car to let us know someone was missing. I didn't pay much attention and drove off, Harley later admitted to me that he knew Mark was going to stay on the base. I would have fired him for it but I needed the workers so we all just said we'd keep quiet about it. The base investigators came and talked to us, we just said we didn't know he slipped off. I'm telling you this at risk to our jobs so keep it to yourselves."

"We'll be discrete, thank you for that, do you know what he was up to?"

"None of my men had any real idea what he was doing. Ken Logan said he thought Mark had seen something and he was going to check on it so he could pass it on to the newspapers and maybe get some money for it. Mark was always trying for an extra buck. I think he went into the wrong area and got shot. The base is covering it up for some reason."

"Now, does the government do stupid things like that?" I said.

Fred broke a smile, "Yeah, they are evil when it comes down to it. Okay, I don't know what Mark was up to, but I do know Mark didn't deserve to die for some stupid secrets that don't amount to a hill of beans for people to worry about. That base runs tests on planes and jets and secret spy planes. Like it's so important to hide it all from the world. Maybe if the world knew what we had, it may scare the pants off some of the evil axis as Georgie Bush said. He at least wanted to bomb the hell out of the enemy."

"I'm not going to debate the worthiness of Bush's administration, I'm concerned about the little boy sitting in the tree house behind his late father's home. He is the loser here, and I want to find out for him why his father had to die. I may need your help, can you?"

Fred stood for a short while taking all what I said into his head. He looked to the back of Louise's trailer where he could see the tree house in the only tree on the property, where Mitch was sitting in the doorway, looking down at the ground.

"Mr.Richards, I don't know what I can do to help you. I'm up against the federal government and they are a lot bigger than you. But Mark was a good guy, I'll do what I can, even if it means losing my job out there. What the hell, may as well take a stand against the men who murder innocent people."

**

Chapter 6

"Thank you, Fred. We're only trying to get to the bottom of this crime. I'll be in touch about our investigation. Maybe we won't have to involve you, I'll let you know."

He thanked me, turned back to his trailer, and went inside leaving us alone. I looked to Buck as he was just standing; staring at the trailer that Fred had gone into. He looked to me, "That man is troubled, he's holding something back, I can just feel it."

I knew Buck's instincts were usually on target, I had to wonder if Fred knew more than he was telling. We wouldn't know until it came out in the wash as they say. I was wondering who they were, I heard a lot about they say, but never really knew who they were. Were they experts in every field, they always knew according to everyone else. Oh, well. Now I was confused, so I stopped thinking about it.

I turned to Louise and asked, "This Harley Musken, do you know him?"

"Yes, he's a friend of Marks, was a friend, he hangs out at the bar inside the A'Le'Inn down the road. There's a small motel there also, if you are staying the night. I'd put you up but we really don't have the room."

"That's fine, I like my privacy. Do you think he'd be there now?"

"When isn't he there is what you should ask. I'm sure you can find him sitting at his favorite stool at the end of the bar. He's big, red beard and hair down to his shoulder blades. He looks like a biker."

Buck snorted and said, "One of my people."

We walked back to the trailer and I excused ourselves to go get a room and see if we can talk to Harley. We drove down the road that the sign said was the "Extraterrestrial Highway" and came to the A'Le'Inn. A great play on words. It was a large white building with various signs and pictures about aliens painted around the sides. Off the side was a tow truck with a flying saucer hanging from the crane. There were five cars parked out front, we parked next to them and went into the building. As we came through the door we could hear laughter and music was playing soft and low. To the left were tables for eating and to the right was the bar. There were about ten patrons in different areas of the room, Buck and I went to the bar to a woman who was tending.

"Greetings gents, what can I get you today?" she said rather pleasantly.

"How about a room if you have one?" I asked.

"Yep, we have one to let, over night or longer?"

"Not sure, but definitely over night, maybe longer."

"I'll get someone to set it up for you, would you like a drink to cool off from your trip?"

"That would be nice; I'll have a Pepsi if you carry it and a Sprite for my friend."

"Coming up." She went off to get the drinks; I looked down the bar and saw a man fitting the description of Harley. Buck saw him also and went down to him. I let Buck take the lead, since he had the biker look to him, I would probably get a negative reaction from Harley.

"Excuse me, are you Harley Musken?"

"Yeah, who's asking?" he said gruffly.

I came up behind Buck with our drinks and Buck gave the man his wide grin and said, "Louise Huston said we could find you here. Can we talk?"

Harley eyed Buck for a couple seconds, "Why did Louise send you to me?"

Buck sat on the stool next to the man, I sat next to Buck.

"My friend and I are here on a secret mission, can we trust you?"

Now he squinted his eyes at Buck, I thought he might take a swing at him but just said, "There's enough secrets around this damn place, what's one more. Is this about Mark?"

"If you can keep it to yourself, I'd appreciate it. We are private investigators from out of Las Vegas. Louise hired us to find out what really happened to Mark. We were told you may have known what Mark was up to the day he was killed."

Harley sat for about a full minute looking around, rubbing his face and beard before he spoke. "Let's go take a table and talk." He stood and went to a table on the other side of the room. We followed.

Buck spoke, "I'm Buck Carson, this is my associate Jim Richards, he's the brains, I'm the brawn. You ride bike?"

"How do you think I got my name?" he chuckled and then, "I got a Harley Roadmaster, my baby. What you got?"

"Harley 94 Ultra Classic, Shriner Edition," Buck said with pride.

"Nice. Now what can I do for you fellows?"

I spoke, "We're in need of finding out what happened the day Mark jumped the bus and then turned up dead. Do you know what that was about?"

He started looking sad, thinking, "I was called by Mark two nights before that fateful day and he asked if I could drive him home the next day. He was going to leave his car and had a plan to make some quick cash. He didn't tell me what, I asked. He said it was something he didn't want to get me involved in, could be dangerous. On the last morning when he would stay behind, I was to drive

43

him to the base parking and then after work leave without him. I knew there was going to be trouble, you don't mess with those Area 51 people. If I had known he was going to get killed, I would have stopped him then and there. Damn."

"Do you know why he had to leave his car, why not just drive himself in that morning?"

"I don't know, he said something about something happening to his car overnight and he had to leave it there."

"Maybe someone was putting something in the car?"

"I had that thought, but he wouldn't say more, he didn't want me to get in trouble if it fell apart. Mark was like that, he'd fall on a grenade for his friends.

"Anything else you can think of to help?" I asked.

"Nope, not much more to tell. He didn't confide in me about it, so I didn't ask."

I took out my business card and handed it to him. "We're going to be staying here for a day or so, call if you remember or hear anything, please."

"If it will help find out what happened, I'll call right away." I thanked him and he got up and went back to the bar. Buck and I just sat thinking.

A youngish woman came up and said our room was ready. I thanked her and she led us out back where the rooms were. They were small but pleasant, Buck said he'd go get our suitcases and left. I pulled my cell phone and hoped there was reception for it, there was. I called Penny and she came on.

"Alien central. This call is being recorded so we can track you down and probe your brain."

"Funny. We are here and have seen no saucers yet, oh wait, we saw one, hanging from the back of a tow truck. Must have broken down in the desert."

"You're at the A'Le'Inn I presume."

"Yes we are, how did you know?" There's that damn telepathy again.

"I talked to one of the crew at the studio and mentioned you were going alien chasing and he said he goes up there a couple times a year with some tour group here in Vegas. They take you to as close as you can get without being shot to watch the base, hoping to see some saucers flying. He told me about the town and the A'Le'Inn."

"It's good that you are researching; maybe I can use your info for my case."

"I'll keep you posted. Now what's up?"

"I just wanted to hear your voice and make sure that my cell phone works out here. How's it going with Jessie?"

Area 51 Murders

"We're having a good time, Willy is all worked up that Jessie is here. We raided the mall and are now just arranging our purchases. How's it out there?"

"This place is really deserted, they don't even get television."

"My God, how are you going to survive?"

"I'll rent some porn on DVD, and think of you."

"You better think of me while watching porn, buster. Any good clues yet?"

"Nope, we just started, talked to the wife and the victim's boss, and a friend, but nothing popping up. I'll let you know in my reports back to the home planet. Alien agent 3.2 over and out." I laughed and hung up.

Buck came in with the suitcases, followed by a man in a sheriff's uniform. "Look what I picked up out front," Buck said with a grin.

"Sheriff, what can we do for you?" I asked.

"Just a courtesy call, I heard that some big city P.I.'s were in town. Just wanted to be sure you're not going to stir up any trouble."

"Now where might you have heard that? I'm sure Louise Huston wouldn't have called you. We've only been in town about an hour and only talked to Harley and Fred. Maybe one of them is concerned about what we may find," I said.

The sheriff stood quietly, then I said, "Look sheriff, we're not here to step on any toes, Louise Huston hired us to find out what happened to Mark Huston. I'd appreciate it if we can all be friends on this."

**

Chapter 7

"Well, I don't want Louise to be hurt, or taken to the cleaners by you gentlemen."

"Sheriff, I'm not even charging Louise for this case, I'm doing it to help her. I do things like that. You can call Captain Weber, Lieutenant Lynn Carter or Sergeant Frank DeAngelo of the Las Vegas Metro Police if you need our references. Or you can call Harold Kettering of the FBI, he'll vouch for us also. I have their numbers handy. Again I'm just trying to help the woman and her son to get a little closure, I'm not going to try and stir up any hornets' nest."

He stood again silently watching me, then he took off his sunglasses, cowboy hat and smiled. "All right fellas, I'll take you at your word, now what have you found out so far?"

"Basically nothing, oh, I'm Jim Richards and this is my associate Buck Carson." I offered my hand, he shook it then Buck's. He said his name was Billy Davis. I continued, "We've probably gotten as much from Fred and Harley as anyone could without torture. Do you know anything about the incident?"

Area 51 Murders

He reached back and closed the door to the room then turned to me and said, "Mark was a good friend of mine, I've tried to find out what I could, the Lincoln County Sheriff's office works closely with the base security, but they are stonewalling us. I can see it and don't like it. Now if you and your associate here find out anything, I'd really appreciate the info. I just happen to drive out here to see how Louise was holding up, just after you two left her home and she told me about you and your exploits in Vegas, I'll say I'm a little impressed. You can take on vigilante killers but the government crazies out on that base should scare you."

"Thanks for the warning, sheriff, I've already been warned by cops and FBI agents, I'm not taking it lightly. Are these men as bad as they make them out to be?"

"Usually when they catch a trespasser they turn them over to us, we deal with them. We'll lock them up for a night then turn them out with a stern warning. Base security has signs posted all over that say "Top Secret Military Facility, Keep Out, Use of Deadly Force Authorized" and they will back it up. They carry big guns and lots of spy equipment to keep intruders out."

"I guess we have our work cut out for us. If I wanted to speak to someone on the base, who might that be?"

"If you're lucky, you can look up Major Colin Rickson, he's the guy who investigates things that are wonky out there. But he's not easy to reach, he doesn't like wasting time on fools. I'm not saying you guys are fools, but they think that way. I'll see if I can get you a meet and greet with him, it's worth a try and if you know someone in the FBI, wouldn't hurt to put in a word that you are going to try to get on the base, just in case you disappear."

That worried me.

~~*~~

Back in Vegas, Trapper was sitting in Samantha's apartment relaxing over a glass of wine. It was still afternoon but Trapper could handle one glass. Sam was sitting next to him with her head on his broad shoulders.

"I'll tell you all I know about my brother being gone. Day before yesterday he asked me if he could borrow ten grand, he knew I was good for it. I asked him why and he said it was personal, I said I couldn't give him that much money without an explanation. He got all upset and started to demand the cash, saying I owed it to him for raising me after our parents died. I laughed and said, 'look how I turned out, a former call girl and now a bookie'. Yep he raised me good. He got mad and stormed out of my business, I haven't seen him since."

"Does your brother gamble?"

"No, he thinks it's for fools who want to part with their money fast. I can't think of anything he would need that much money for, I've racked my brain. He's never gone very long without calling. He's a good brother and I should have given him the money, but I just wanted to know he wasn't in trouble." She picked her head off Trapper's shoulder to take a sip of wine, then she got up and went to the kitchen. She came back with a bag of Cheetos.

"Ah, the way to my heart, Cheetos. Does your brother have many friends in town?" He asked as he took a handful of the snack.

"He has a couple friends who work with him at the Club Venus, he's a bouncer and bartender. They lived together in an apartment off Sahara and Paradise; I'll give you the address. I called them and they said they haven't seen him either, that's when I called you."

"Well, I'll need to talk to his friends, maybe they can tell me something that I can go on. Now before I go out and do my Sherlock impersonation, how about we discuss my fee?"

"Can I take it out in trade?" She gave Trapper a demure smile and then they went to the bedroom.

~~*~~

"Sheriff, have there been any other incidences happening lately, crime increases or missing people?" I asked.

"Yeah, now that you mention that, Darryl Longhorn has been missing for about a week. The locals figured he left town, since he was such a loser and couldn't hold down a job. Not that there are many jobs out here, so they thought he just up and left. I haven't been by his place to see for myself, just heard it through the grapevine that he may have left for better pastures." He stood thinking, "Maybe a good idea to go see if he's really gone. Care to tag along?"

"Sure, if you don't mind?"

"Keep up, I drive fast," he said with a smile. "This country is so far apart you have to occasionally break the speed limits, even we look aside."

We went to Trapper's Jeep and followed the sheriff's patrol car out the highway and up northward. He finally arrived at a long dirt drive off the road and went on for a half mile until we came to a trailer sitting by itself in the desert. Buck and I got out and went to the sheriff as he stood studying the trailer.

"Wow, this guy lives like a hermit I presume?" Buck said.

"Darryl is a Native American, he doesn't mind living without the trappings of civilization." He went to the door of the trailer and banged on it. He received no response.

The sheriff tried the door; it was locked. He went around the trailer trying to look in the windows, but the shades were drawn all around. We came back to the front, the sheriff went to the door, sniffing.

"Do you fellas smell gas? I smell gas, maybe a leak. I think I'm in my within authority to break in and check to see if all is well."

Area 51 Murders

I smiled knowing he was using the excuse to enter the trailer; I wasn't going to cite law for him. He broke the glass on the door and reached in to open it from inside.

"You gentlemen wait out here, just in case." He entered and was inside for a couple minutes when he called for us to enter. The trailer was trashed; someone had gone through it.

"You fellas are the big city private eyes, what do you think?"

"I'd say there was foul play here, do you concur?"

"I'd say that was a pretty good assumption, Darryl was never much of a housekeeper but this is not his doing. I've had to bring Darryl home a couple time after drinking too much at the A'Le'Inn, so I'm familiar with is home habits." He was rummaging through the mess, looking for something I presumed.

I started to pick up papers strewn all over the floor, trying to get a handle on Darryl by what the papers told me. There were a few letters from the Office of Indian Affairs, mostly about Darryl's complaints to them about poor conditions in the county for Native Americans. I found a few old tickets for public nuisance, being drunk and causing trouble. I found nothing much that told me anything.

Buck was sitting on the arm of a chair by the front door when he said that a car was approaching. The sheriff went to the door and then out. The car was government, labeled Air Force on the side. The car stopped just short of the trailer and a man in uniform got out and came to the sheriff. There was one other man, wearing a sidearm and an arm patch identifying him as military police. He stepped out of the passenger side and stood by the car, waiting.

"Hello sheriff, I'm Captain Les D'Amico, U.S Air Force adjutant to Major Rickson, is Darryl Longhorn here?"

The sheriff studied the man for a minute before speaking, "What's the Air Force need with Darryl?"

"He recently had been involved with a breach of the base and we are looking for him. He was detained on the base but somehow managed to escape, we are looking for him."

"Well, so am I. He seems to be missing here too. His trailer was trashed and he's not in the county as far as his friends are concerned. You say he was detained on the base?"

"Yes he managed to get into the base, how we are not sure, but he was captured in one of the buildings, but managed to get away and was caught trying to climb one of the fences around a secure building on the base. He was taken to our infirmary to treat his wounds from the concertina wire of the fence; but when I went to see him the next morning he had escaped. You say you don't know where he went."

"Nope, you sure he left the base, maybe he's still hiding out there."

The Captain looked back to the MP, who got back into the car, and then looked back to the sheriff, "Good point, if he is we'll find him." He saluted then left.

**

Chapter 8

"Well, that's interesting. Now you at least know where Darryl has been. Do you think Darryl will try to contact you for any reason?" I asked.

"Darryl and I get along on a professional level; he gets drunk, I take him home. Darryl still doesn't trust the white man's law. If he does try to contact me, it will be for a serious matter. Not that being caught on Area 51 and wanted by the Air Force spooks isn't serious. I guess time will tell, at least I know he's on the loose."

The sheriff went to the door, looked at it and then from under the trailer he pulled out a piece of wood big enough to cover the broken window. He asked me to hold it while he went to his car and got a hammer and some nails from his truck. He came back, nailed the sheet of wood to the inside of the door, then closed the door.

"That should keep the wildlife out at least, but nothing is safe from humans," he said.

I liked his simple philosophy. He seemed like a decent guy, I guess I could count on him to help. He stood surveying the property, like he was waiting for Darryl to suddenly pop up, he didn't.

"Well, gentlemen, I'll let you get back to your investigating. I'll see if I can arrange a visit with Major Rickson, I don't guarantee much. I'll let you know." He went to his patrol car and drove off, leaving Buck and I standing by the trailer. I tried the door and found it unlocked. I didn't know if the sheriff forgot or was letting us take another look at the inside. Buck gave me a nod and we went in.

We spent about a half hour digging through the mess, I didn't have much hope of finding anything, someone did a pretty good job of searching before us. I was turning pictures on the wall when I found a piece of paper taped to the back of a photo of the Hoover Dam. I pulled it off and opened the paper. It was a hand drawn map of the property around Area 51 showing some kind of drainage system going out to the desert. I know when they get rain in the desert it can become a flash flood situation; I saw it in Vegas. Which is why they have drain canals around the city. I showed it to Buck and then folded it back up, putting it in my coat pocket.

"That may be how Darryl got into the base. Good to have for later, if we need it," I said.

"You aren't thinking of breaking onto the base now are you?" Buck asked with a smile, "That would be illegal, I like it."

We locked up the trailer and headed back to town.

Area 51 Murders

~~*~~

Trapper was driving up the strip from Sam's apartment in one of the luxury high rises. If the management only knew who their tenant was, they might object. Her front for her bookie operation was a hair salon; it had many employees and lots of clients. The back room also had many employees and lots of clients who placed bets on sports and horse racing across the country. It was illegal of course, but this is Sin City and gambling is the major attraction. The casinos didn't like competition from entrepreneurs opening up shops around the city. The police usually looked the other way unless there was a complaint by a patron who may have felt cheated, but the bookies usually kept their clients happy and the cops off their doorstep. Sam was also a favorite of many of the higher up cops from her days as a high paid escort, so she was fairly safe from arrest.

Trapper was heading to the Venus Club, a popular nightclub for the gay community. It featured great music and nightly drag shows which brought in many customers from around the world visiting in town for a good night out. There were four other gay clubs in town, but this one was the favored. It was classy and lots of flashing lights on the dance floor.

Trapper had been in this club only once before with a couple of his cop friends, who didn't admit it out loud, but where of the gay persuasion. Trapper was comfortable with his friends but wasn't particularly crazy about dancing with men. So he would dance with some of the really attractive transgendered women that frequented the clubs. He just pretended to be in the company of real females and that was that. Never a slow dance, ever, but the DJ usually spun only the hard driving beat of disco type music.

Trapper arrived and parked. He went in, paid the cover charge and went into the club proper. It was slow tonight but it was early yet, so he went to the bar and asked the woman behind the bar if she knew where Tommy was.

She smiled and said, "I'm Tommy, but you can call me Tammy, whatcha need hon?"

Trapper was at first surprised but didn't show it. "I'm a friend of Samantha Hathaway, you know her brother Phillip?"

"Oh hell yes stud, he's a favorite around here, but he goes by Phyllis. You haven't seen her by chance? She's been AWOL for a couple days."

Trapper smiled, suddenly wondering if Sam knew of her brother's lifestyle. She wasn't dumb, but sometimes a person may not know their loved ones well enough.

"He... I mean she, is missing and her sister asked me to find him, her. I'm a private investigator. Can you tell me anything that may help to find Phyllis?"

"Well, I think you need to talk to Mandy, she is closer to Phyllis than I was, she probably can help you."

"Where might I find Mandy?"

Area 51 Murders

"She's on stage in five minutes; can I get you a drink?"

~~*~~

Buck and I were wearing out and hungry so we went to the A'Le'Inn to get lunch. We sat and the same youngish woman who readied our room came up and handed us menus. We had to try the Alien burger so we asked for that and fries. She went off and I sat looking around the room. Harley was on his stool at the bar; he saw us and saluted with his beer bottle.

We had our burgers, delicious they were and then we finished with a beer for me and Sprite for Buck. We suddenly were joined by a rather plump, fairly attractive woman with long brown hair tied back with a red ribbon. She smiled and took a drink from the bottle she brought with her.

"Hope you don't mind but I need to talk to you. I heard you are possibly looking for a reason why Mike Huston was killed. I may be able to help." She slurred her words and took another swig of the beer, then gave a little belch. She said, "Excuse me," and put the bottle down. She sat staring at the bottle, studying it for what, I didn't know.

"You say you have some info for us?" I said.

She looked startled, then I realized she was blotto, beer soaked. Her eyes glazed and she mumbled, "Yeah, I know why he was killed." Then her head dropped to the table, she passed out.

Buck said, "Does everyone here drink into a stupor?"

"Harley can hold his beer," I said looking over to him. He turned on the stool, saw our dilemma and came over.

"Molly isn't bothering you is she?" he said.

"We don't know, she passed out before she could bother us. She said she may know why Mark was killed. Is there a place we can take her to sober up?" I asked.

"Yeah, hey Pat you got a room open for about an hour or two?" he yelled to the woman behind the bar. "We need to sober Molly up. Again."

We had Molly in the room and the waitress brought us a pot of coffee and a bottle of some stuff that said it would cure hangovers. I was trying to bring her around, but she drifted in and out. I sprinkled water on her face and that made her mad. I jumped back before she could punch me and then she looked at us with wide eyes.

"What the hell am I doing in here, and who are you people." I presumed she was referring to Buck and me.

Harley sat next to her and said, "Molly, take it easy, we just brought you here to get sobered up. You passed out in the bar."

She was still watching Buck and me, then she said, "I remember, you are the dicks who are looking for Mark's killer."

I never liked the term dick when it referred to detectives, mostly an archaic term and slightly offensive now days. I bravely moved closer and sat on the table next to the bed she was now sitting on. She still looked like she would pass out but she held up better.

"Yes, we are. Do you know something that may help with this?"

"Mark and I were buds, we knew each other from when we was kids. He married Louise and I didn't like it but what can you do? Mark still talked to me when he'd come down here to drink. He told me of his plan to make lots of money from the base. He said he had a contact on the base and they were going to take something off the base that was worth a lot of money. I think his contact on the base killed him, to take all the money."

**

Chapter 9

"Molly, when did Mark tell you all this?" I asked.

"The day before he was killed. He was worried about going in and doing the job but he needed the money. That was the last I saw of him." Her head drooped and I left her alone. I stood and went to Buck standing by the door.

"We need to talk to someone on the base. Just to see what they know so far. If they even tell us."

"It's worth a try; you need to talk to the sheriff again," Buck said.

I pulled out the sheriff's card he gave me earlier and went out of the room. Outside the building, I dialed the number on the card and about three rings later, the sheriff answered.

"Sheriff, this is Jim Richards, we just talked to a woman named Molly and she said she talked to Mark the day before he was killed. She said he was involved with someone on the base who was trying to take something off the base. I'd like to talk to that Major if you can get us in?"

"I already called and they are going to get back to me with a time to go see the man. I'll call you so just sit tight." I thanked him and hung up. I told Buck what he said and we went back in the room. Molly was now sitting on a straight back chair by a writing desk; Harley was trying to get her to drink the coffee.

"Molly, is there anything else Mark may have said about what they were trying to take off the base?" I asked.

"No, he just told me he had someone who worked on the base and had access to something important. Something that would be worth a lot of money to the right people. I don't know what it was."

"Thank you for that. It may help our investigation. Harley, Mark never told you anything about this when you drove him into the base?"

"Well, I asked why he had to leave his car and he said someone was going to do something to it, but he wouldn't tell me what. I didn't push it, too many secrets on that base that I didn't want to know. Damn place scares me."

~~*~~

Trapper sat back in the chair by the stage, watching Mandy doing a great impersonation of Reba McEntire singing 'Fancy' and 'I'm A Survivor', she was very good for a female impersonator Trapper thought. After she finished she came off the stage and Trapper went to her standing by the bar.

"Excuse me?" he said.

"You're excused cutie, what may I do for you and I hope it's what I'm thinking."

Trapper smiled and said, "I'm looking for Phillip, or Phyllis, do you know where she may be?"

"What do you want with her? You better not be one of those thugs who have been bothering her. I'll kick the crap out of you if you are."

Trapper believed she could do it, even if she did look like Reba. "No, I'm a private investigator working for Phyllis' sister, she's concern because she doesn't know where Phyllis is. Can you help?"

She stood staring at Trapper then finally spoke, "Let's go find a quiet table and talk."

~~*~~

My cell phone rang and I went out of the room again to answer. The caller ID said private, but I answered anyway.

"Hello," I said.

"Richards, this is Sheriff Davis, I guess the military people are hot to find out what you want with this situation, they want you to come out immediately, as they said. I just got a call from that nice Captain fella who we met in the desert by Darryl's trailer. He said to come to the main gate at the base and he'd meet you there. Do you know the way?"

Area 51 Murders

"I have no idea how to get there," I said.

The sheriff gave me quick directions to the road leading to the gate and said to have the guard at the gate call the Captain when we got there. I thanked him and hung up. I called to Buck, explaining the conversation and we went to the car. I followed the directions and we did end up at a gate guarded by four heavily armed military personnel and lots of cameras. I told the guard who we wanted to speak to and he called in. He told us to park in the small lot on the side and wait.

We met Captain D'Amico at the gate as he pulled up in an older style military jeep. He waved to us and we went to him.

"Good afternoon gentlemen, the Major is waiting for you, He's rather impatient but willing to hear you out," he said and pointed to the seats, we climbed in and he drove off. He took a rather obscure way around; it was mostly behind large buildings so we couldn't see much of the base. He pulled up to the back of a large five-story office building and got out; we followed. He led us into the building and took us to a desk being manned by a large man wearing what looked like desert combat fatigues. The man gave us badges stating that we were guests and told us to clip them to our shirts. We followed the Captain down a number of hallways and up two flights of stairs to a door labeled "Intelligence". We entered and there was a woman behind a desk in uniform. I could never remember if it was a WAC or WAF designation or if they even still use the term, I'd have to ask.

"Airman Holt, we're here to see the Major." The Captain spoke to the woman as she pushed a button and lifted a phone. She said to go in and the Captain took us to the door marked 'Major Colin Rickson, Special Investigations.' We entered the large office and I saw a man standing behind a rather large mahogany desk, covered by stacks of papers and file holders. He gave us a steely eye, and said to sit. We did. Buck sat back by the door, I took the chair by his desk, Captain D'Amico stood at parade rest until the Major sat at his desk told the Captain to get lost.

I had to stifle a laugh at his command to the Captain, I could see he was a no nonsense person.

Major Rickson was an older man, he had steely blue eyes, and wire rimmed glasses. He looked as though at one time that he may have had a beautiful head of blonde hair, but it was thinning now, cut short of course. He sported a very straight nose, but not aquiline or narrow. I could tell he was in better shape than most younger men, fit and trim. When he was standing, I could tell he was about 5'10", my height, but he seems to hold himself well and straight, so he seemed larger. I liked him as soon as I sized him up.

"Now, I'm doing this out of courtesy to the Lincoln County Sheriff, he's a good man, and spoke highly of you two," he said. "I don't like wasting time and breath so state your case. You're here about the death of Mark Huston, correct?"

"Yes we are, sir. I'm Jim Richards and the man behind me is Buck Carson, we are private investigators. Mark's widow hired us to find out what happened to her husband."

Area 51 Murders

"Doesn't she think we can handle it?" he barked.

"I'm sorry Major, but this base has so many rumors and secrets, she wasn't sure if she could get an honest answer. She needs closure, not conspiracy theories."

The Major eyed me for a moment and said, "Fair enough, yes Area 51 has a lot of goings on that we don't like people to know about. But we try to be fair about things like murder on our property. Mark Huston was on the base doing something illegal as we have determined so far, what it was, we aren't sure of. Do you have a theory?"

"Well he did confide in a friend about something he was going to try and get off the base, something he thought he could make money with. I'm sure you know that the area is not wealthy, he did it out of desperation for his family. It was also stated that there was an accomplice on the base helping to do the deed. My source thinks Mark was murdered by this person. I don't suppose you might know what they may have planned on stealing?"

"Mr. Richards, this base does many experiments, studies and research, so any one thing could be subject to being sold to outside factions. We have already considered this."

"Is the body of Mark going to be released anytime soon? His widow would like to bury him properly."

He sat for a moment and said, "I'll see about getting the body sent to her soon, I'll try and have it cleared by tomorrow. I'm sure they are finished with him. No sense in making the poor woman suffer any further."

I noticed a rather large rubber stamp on his desk, it was turned enough so I could read the backward words, it was just one word in big bold, block letters, it said "BULLSHIT". I asked the Major what was the significance of the stamp.

He cracked a small smile now and said, "Over the years I have received many correspondence from the Pentagon, I don't suffer stupidity well, so I would write across the papers in big words, 'bullshit' and send them back. One Christmas the Pentagon sent me a present. This rubber stamp," he said as he picked it up, "They said it would look more official than hand lettering. I've used it many times for many internal and outside letters," he said, keeping a small grin on his face, more of a smirk, this usually makes people uncomfortable, but I found it rather funny.

I said, "I'm glad to see they have a sense of humor. Major, I'm not going to be interfering in this matter but I really would appreciate if you keep me filled in on what happened to Mark, for his wife and son."

"I'm afraid we can't do much because we have no way to find out who this inside man is without a little subterfuge. I've contacted the office of Homeland Security to see if they can do an undercover investigation, since we felt at first this could be a terrorist attempt on the base. They are stretched thin, so their attempts to work the case would be delayed until they can free up some agents. That may take weeks if not months. By then this could be an incident of unknown proportions."

"Major, I may have a possible solution if I could tell you about it," I said. He listened.

Chapter 10

Trapper and Mandy went to the far corner of the club where there were fewer people and sat at a candlelit table. Mandy was a very attractive female impersonator, looking amazingly like Reba McEntire, even up close. She wore a red sequined dress with a low cleavage-showing cut revealing what looked like full breasts. They were either implants or a clever use of padding.

"You say that Phyllis is missing? Is this from her sister Sam?"

"Yes, I'm a good friend of Sam's, we're sort of dating. She asked me if I could find out what happened to her brother. She didn't mention Phillip's gender preference."

"Phyllis was very private about her identity. I think she never mentioned this to the sister. I'm surprised the sister didn't put two and two together and figure Phyllis was transgendered. She never hid the fact."

"I've known many gay and transgendered people and most hide the fact from the people closest to them. Fear of rejection or hate, take your pick."

"I do know that, it was many years before I could even open up about my identity. So what do you need to know about Phyllis?"

"Well, do you know where she is?"

"No, I haven't seen her in about two days. We live in the same apartment, but we have different lives and different timetables, so we don't see much of each other. I have a boyfriend and I do stay at his place frequently, so not seeing Phyllis is no big thing. But I have noticed an absence in the apartment; you know clothes lying around or food missing, little things like that."

"You mentioned when I first asked about Phyllis that she had some thugs bothering her?"

"Yes, there were a couple of strong arms coming in and asking for Phyllis, about the week before you say she came up missing. They were rather rude about her not being in and wanted to know where she lived, we don't give out that info and they didn't like it. Us queens can be mean too, so they left."

"Tell me about Phyllis' life."

"I know she is a private person, she was planning on undergoing the transition, so she was trying to raise the money."

"Transition? You mean she is going to undergo sexual reassignment surgery?"

"Yes sir, male to female all the way. That should be a sign for the sister to know about Phyllis' preference."

"I would say so. Is there anywhere else you know of where Phyllis may be staying?"

"I wish I could say, but we weren't that close. We lived in an apartment with one other tranny but she's never around. So I hardly knew my roommates. Shame isn't it? So close yet so far."

"Yep, like life." Trapper gave Mandy his card, "If you hear from her, let me know please. The men who came in, did they say anything that would give me a lead to find them?"

"As they were leaving, one of them said that Ricky won't like hearing that they couldn't find her. That's all I got out of it."

Trapper thought on that, he'd have to check if there were any mob connections to a Ricky. "Mandy, thank you and you are one hell of a performer." Trapper stood and said, "I'll have to bring a couple of my friends to catch your show. Thanks."

He left her and went back to his car. He pulled his cellphone and called his friend LVMPD Detective Josh Harper. "Hey Josh, Will here, got a minute?"

"Crime stops for you buddy, what's up?"

"I need to know if you heard of someone in the system named Ricky, he has a couple goons who go in search for people. Why for, I don't know yet."

"Could be Ricky Collissi, minor hood and suspected loan shark. They call him Rancid Ricky, his business stinks and so does his hygiene. He has some boys who collect for him, nothing we can pin on him so far, but he's being watched."

"Well, that fits. I got a case where a person tried to borrow a large sum of money from a relative, maybe to pay Rancid Ricky back. Got any idea where I can find him?"

"You don't want to go chasing him alone, not a good idea. I'm not doing anything at the moment, I'll meet you at Carl's Jr. on Maryland and we'll grab a bite to eat, then go chase bad guys."

"Sounds good to me, see you there." Trapper smiled and hung up.

~~*~~

I finished laying out my plan as the Major sat stoney faced and then he looked beyond me; I hoped he was thinking over my plot.

"Mr. Richards, what you propose is dangerous to say the least. If this person is a killer, you could be in danger also."

"I've been in worse situations. Besides, I'd have my bodyguard Buck to watch my back," I said as I could hear Buck snickering behind me.

"I'm glad you have faith in your partner, I've always depended on my troops to cover my ass too. I'll think about what you propose and get back to you after I make a few calls. Do you think you could pull it off?"

"It can't hurt to try, and catch a criminal in the trying."

"Before I allowed you come in to talk to me I did some calling around, I know about your reputation in crime fighting. Impressive list of serial killers you have caught." He paused still thinking. "Alright, I'll contact you." He pushed a button, spoke into the desk intercom, and asked for the Captain to come back in. He did and the Major stood thanking us for coming and told the Captain to take us back to our cars.

"I'd say that went well, but I'm not sure if it did," Buck said as we were driving back to the A'Le'Inn.

"At least they didn't zap our brains with their mind probes." I laughed.

"Don't make fun; they may have while we sat in the office. You don't know what they are capable of doing."

"Very true, they can spy on us from a satellite; they may be watching us right now."

Buck stuck his head and arm out his window and then gave the finger to the sky. "There, let them sit on that."

It was now almost five o'clock, it was a very busy day. We got back to the A'Le'Inn and we were both totally worn down, age has its pitfalls and I didn't have my nap. I was getting used to not having an afternoon nap; I was too busy playing detective anymore to have a nap. But it did make for some better sleeping at night.

We went back in to have a quick dinner and I saw the sheriff sitting at the bar next to Harley. He saw us come in and came over to the table we were heading for.

"So how was the talk with the big chief?" he said as he sat.

"It went all right. I don't really know much more other than they will be releasing Mark's body in a day or two. I'm sure they'll call you on it. Does this town have any kind of funeral parlor?"

"Hell, they just closed the only gas station in town and you think there may be a funeral parlor? We usually just go dig a hole in the desert and drop the body in," he said as he tried not to smile.

"All right, I'm tired and not thinking straight. So what do you do with the bodies?"

"We ship them to Crystal Springs or Ash Springs; they have all that stuff there. Louise already told me she wants to go to Ash Springs with Mark. I called a funeral parlor there that I've dealt with in the past. It's all arranged as soon as they give us his body."

"Will there be an autopsy?"

"What for, we know he was shot."

"Yes, but things from the body can tell us much more. I'll call the Clark County ME and see if he would like a vacation to come up and look at the remains. He's a friend."

"Sounds like a lot of extra work but if it floats your boat, go ahead. I'll let the funeral home know."

"Thanks Sheriff, now we are going to eat and I'm going to collapse in my bed."

~~*~~

Trapper and Josh went to where Rancid Ricky was being staked out. They snuck up on the surveillance car and Josh banged on the driver side window scaring the crap out of the two detectives inside. The man on the driver's side rolled down the window and yelled, "What the hell do you think this is? I was just about sleeping."

"Shame, you are supposed to be watching Ricky," Josh said.

"Yeah well, he hasn't moved since this morning. His dry cleaning business is booming with customers. Probably everyone is getting their money laundered."

"He's still in there then?"

"As far as I've seen he is, I occasionally see him come out front of the counter and look out the window. Probably watching me watch him."

"Thanks Lloyd, we need to talk to Ricky so watch our backs."

"Will do, and tell him to quit scratching his ass, it looks disgusting."

We walked across the highway and up to the door of the Sunshine Dry Cleaners. We went in and to the counter; a girl asked us if we had clothes to press.

"No but we have some cash to clean," Josh said. "Is Ricky in?"

**

Chapter 11

The counter girl hesitated, then reached under the counter and pushed a button. About two minutes later, a very fat and ugly man came walking out followed by two goons who came around the counter. Josh turned to them and pulled back his jacket exposing his badge and the butt of his P226 Sig Sauer 9mm service pistol. They stopped.

"Gentlemen, what can I do for our Vegas finest cops." Ricky spoke in clipped English.

Josh watched the two thugs go back behind the counter after Ricky gave them a thumb. "We just have a question or two to ask then we'll leave you to your dry cleaning."

Trapper leaned over the counter to Ricky, but pulled back after catching a whiff of his body odor. Trapper wondered how any of his people could work around him. "I just need to know if you know of a person by the name of Phillip Hathaway?"

"Hataway? Nah, never heard of him." He looked to his men and asked, "You boys know dis Hataway?"

Trapper watched their expressions, they looked dumb enough to give a tell. One of the goon's expression said he knew, but he shook his head no. Trapper could see the man's coat open slightly and he saw a handgun tucked into his belt. Trapper pointed to him and asked, "What's your name?"

The goon said "Vito."

Trapper said, "Well, Vito, you got a permit for the gun?"

The man was looking nervous, he started to reach for the weapon, Josh had his Sig out and commanded both men to put their hands up or he'd ventilate them. Lloyd from across the street saw Josh pull the gun and he and his partner came running. They stormed into the building with guns drawn. Josh was around the counter pulling the men to the wall and removing their weapons. Ricky was yelling about police harassment, Trapper told him to shut up.

Josh asked Lloyd's partner to put his handcuffs on Vito; Lloyd put his on the other man. Josh told Lloyd to put them in the car and turned to Ricky. "Now do you know Hathaway?"

"I'll have them out before the day is over."

Josh called on his radio for back up then turned to Ricky, "Yeah, well, since there has been a crime on the premises, illegal weapon possession, we have to check out your building."

"Okay, guys, maybe I knew dis Hataway. What do that mean ta you?"

"Talk quickly before my people get here."

"Dis guy comes to me for a loan, I ask what for, have to be sure my investment is good. He said he needs it fer an operation, health problem. I give it ta him, he don't pay me when he say he would. We go ta look but can't find him. Dat's all I know. Not illegal to give a man money, is it?"

"Illegal only if you demanded exorbitant interest or killed him for it," Trapper said.

"I did neither. I run a good business, I help people."

"Yeah, yeah, my heart breaks." Lloyd came back in and Josh turned to him, "Watch Mr. Collissi so he doesn't do something stupid, like run. Back-up should be here shortly."

"Hey, you said if I talked you'd call off the dogs."

"I didn't say that, I just said to talk fast before my people get here. I make no promises to crooks." Josh smiled at Ricky and then he and Trapper went to the back room.

Area 51 Murders

~~*~~

Buck and I were resting in our room; it was dark except for the lamp on the desk. The room was comfortable, dark wood and wallpaper, early outdoors theme. We had a rollaway bed brought in and Buck and I flipped for it, I won the main bed. Buck grumbled about being too long for the rollaway, I finally gave in to this whining and said he could have the bed.

He was stretched out relaxing as I pulled my cell phone and dialed Penny. She came on after two rings.

"Hey babe, how's life in the big city?" I asked.

"Oh so lonely without you," she said then laughed, I was offended. "Are the aliens behaving?"

"I've been on Area 51, and my mind hasn't been probed; now my butt feels like it was probed."

Her laugh was so nice to my ears; I always love hearing it. "I may be out here for a while longer, this is taking on a bit of a sting and I need to help the government catch the criminal."

"You volunteered to be bait again, didn't you?" she said, I was always amazed how she could read me, "You are such an idiot. If it doesn't kill you, I might."

"I love you too. How's our baby?"

"Willy hasn't asked where you are yet, I think he doesn't care."

"Well, when the dog does talk to you, call the news."

We talked a little longer and then we signed off. I laid down on the rollaway, after I threw the sheets I brought with me on it. I didn't trust any motel room beds, after seeing an expose on the TV about creepy things in motel beds. I was getting comfortable and drifted off. I slept well, but had dreams about big-eyed aliens carrying me off in their saucer.

I woke refreshed early the next morning; country air always does that for me. I was also hungry, country air does that to me also. Buck was already up and in the tiny bathroom getting cleaned up. He finished and I went in, and about choked on the smell. "Thanks Buck, you couldn't take your farts outside."

He roared out loud and said he was sorry, but nature called and he answered.

We were finished and went over to the restaurant bar for breakfast. The place was just about empty, we sat and the same girl came to serve us. I wondered how many hours she worked.

We ate our breakfast and then relaxed; I was reading the newspaper from Crystal Springs, not much going on. My cell phone rang and I answered. It was Captain D'Amico, he asked if we could come back out to the base, the Major wanted to see us. I hung up and looked to Buck, "We have been summoned to alien alley."

Area 51 Murders

As we were getting ready to leave, the sheriff came in and saw us. He came over, "Good morning, fellas. Sleep well?"

"Yes, as a matter of fact, quite well," Buck spoke.

I just smiled and told the sheriff, "We just got a call to go back to the base. If they are responding to my proposal, I may need your help and Fred's. I'll call you later to let you know."

"I'll be waiting for you. Just call," he said and went to the bar to talk to the owner.

Buck and I drove out the same road and came to the gate where the guard had called the Captain. He came out and took us back to the Major's office. The office was empty as Buck and I sat, waiting. The major came in and apologized for making us wait. He said he had things to take care of.

"Mr. Richards, I don't care for uptight idiots. I had a commanding officer once who drove me batty. He was anal about things being just right, his pictures on the walls had to be perfect; his desk was just arranged perfectly. So, every time I would go by his office and he wasn't in, I would go in and make his pictures crooked. It drove him nuts. I have a sense of humor that many find a bit strange, but I amuse myself. I tell you this because I don't want you to think I'm some stuck up bureaucrat, I talked to a number of people about your plan and they didn't like it, but I say bullshit. I'm going to authorize it, but you are on your own if it goes wrong. I'll help you the best I can, but I can't give you backup. So be careful, I don't need more bodies piling up."

"I'll be careful and as I said, Buck will be with me at all times."

"Fine, when can we start this undercover operation?"

"I have to talk to the boss of the crew, but I'm sure he will cooperate. I'm hoping we can come in tomorrow morning. Do we have clearance to work on the base?" I asked.

"I'll authorize it, and have your ID badges at the main gate, have Fred Parnell get your badges when you arrive, I'll need to take pictures of you both for the badges." He called Captain D'Amico back in and the Captain took our pictures with a Polaroid type camera and then went off. "This better go right, we need to stop whoever is doing this before it goes wrong. Something is up and something is going to happen. I'm depending on you two. Now leave before you are seen here to blow your cover." He gave me his card with his personal number, "I case you need me. Thank you Mr. Richards and good luck."

We went out and Captain D'Amico took us back to our car. We drove out to Rachel again and up to Fred Parnell's home. He was in his garage working on some electrical device; it looked like it was a small transformer, probably something for the town's power.

He greeted us and I asked if we could go sit and talk. He led us to his home and we went into his kitchen and sat at the table.

"Fred, we just came off the base after talking to the investigating officer for the murder of Mark. We have been given a green light to do an undercover sting to find the killer of Mark and find out what the whole matter was about. We are coming on the base in the morning along with your men to pretend we are new guys on the crew. The Major has authorized the sting and requested that you cooperate. How's this sound to you?"

"My country calls, I answer. Besides I always wanted to be part of an undercover operation," he said and grinned.

**

Chapter 12

We spent the rest of the afternoon picking Fred's brain for info about the job. He showed us various equipment and items that we would need to pretend we knew something about so we didn't look totally stupid. Fred explained the procedure for doing the job and the people we would come in contact with.

"Since Mark had arranged with our mystery person to take something off the base, it could be someone that hung around your work area, anyone come to mind?" I asked.

"Wow, there were a number of people that worked in the area, there's the construction crew working on the building and there's the guards assigned to make sure we didn't take pictures or steal anything, now that's a laugh. I couldn't pin any one person to being the criminal. Sorry, I just never paid much attention to who my men socialized with."

"That's another thing, lunch time, where did you eat?"

"We ate on the site, they had a picnic table set up in the hanger to keep us together. We all ate in shifts, my men, then the construction workers, then the plumbers if they worked that day, etc. It was hard to socialize when you are being herded around."

"Could the mystery man have met with Mark off the base? Do the base people have to stay on the base or can they come into town?"

"If they do go off the base, they'd take another road that would take them to Crystal Springs, more action there. Rachel is not exactly a hot spot."

"So I've noticed. I'm going to talk to the employees at A'Le'Inn to see if they remember anyone from the base entertaining Mark."

We picked Fred's brain a little longer about the job and arranged to meet him in the morning to follow him out to the base. We left him to his work and went back to the inn.

"Do you have a plan?" asked Buck as we munched on our lunch back at the inn.

"Nope, I'm playing it by ear, my best feature. We'll find out what to expect when we get there and if anyone approaches us."

"What if the bad guy on the base has already taken the stolen goods off the base, he wouldn't want to mess with us then."

"Thanks, I thought about that but was hoping you wouldn't notice."

"Well, it is an option. So if it's a possibility, we may be working on the base forever and never catch the culprit."

"Well, if we don't stir up something after we get there, we'll just pull out and give our apologies. We're not perfect."

"I'm perfect, you may not be, but I am," Buck said quietly as he slurped his soup.

"Yes Buck, you are perfect."

The front door of the inn opened and in walked the sheriff. He sauntered over to us and sat, placing his cowboy hat on the empty chair. "Well fellas, got a call and they are delivering Mark in this afternoon."

"Delivering?" I said.

"Yep, they are dropping him off at my office and I have a suburban to take him to Ash Springs. Is your ME going to take a look?"

"I haven't called him but will shortly. Will the funeral home keep him on ice till he gets here?"

"I can have it arranged. Let me know what your man says about coming in."

"Sheriff, can we talk to the employees of the inn to find out if anyone from the base was friendly with Mark in here?"

"You ask and I do." He stood and went to the bar and talked to the woman tending, then came back to us. The woman went around the building gathering the three employees and having them come to us. I stood and asked them to pull up chairs. They did.

"For those who may not know, I'm here investigating Mark's death for his wife. I just need to know if any of you saw Mark in here with any base personnel getting friendly, maybe talking quietly and secretively."

The two women and one young man sat staring at me; they looked like deer in headlights. "I'm not going to bite, just talk to me."

"Well, I might bite if someone doesn't say something," The sheriff growled.

They looked to him, then to me, the youngest woman who waited on us, cleared her throat and spoke. "I remember a man talking to Mark the day before he... died. The man was definitely base personnel. Every time I would go near the table they would hush up."

"What did he look like?" I asked.

"He was thin, very thin, and had a pointy nose. He had dull red hair, almost like a chestnut. When he stood he was a bit taller than me, I'm five-eight."

"You didn't hear anything, a name or some bit of conversation they may have said?"

"They were arguing part of the time, not loud but heated. I thought the military guy was going to punch Mark once. I stood back watching to be sure he didn't or I would have clocked him with my tray." She held up a heavy brown tray for drinks, it looked like it might do some damage.

"Anyone else?" I asked. I received no response. The sheriff cleared his throat and they jumped. The young man looked nervous and then said, "I was cleaning the table next to them and I heard Mark call the guy Dylan as they argued about money. They realized I was there and watched me finish. I finished quickly and left, the Dylan guy made me nervous, he looked evil."

"Freddy evil or Hitler evil?" I asked.

The man gave me a blank stare and said, "Who?"

"Freddy from 'Nightmare on Elm Street' and … never mind, you're too young to know. So, you didn't like his looks, I'll take that in consideration," I said.

The sheriff was snickering, I gave him a look and he stopped. "You have anything more to say sheriff?"

"Yeah, Lori, you haven't said anything. I know you like to scope out people so what did you see?" He was speaking to the woman who sat quietly, not talking like the others.

"I don't know anything, sheriff. Well, maybe I saw the car he drove, a foreign car, small, round, it was funny looking."

"Round, like a Volkswagon Beetle?" I asked.

She gave me a blank stare. "Don't schools teach anything about history?" I pulled out my Palm TX and went through the pictures searching for a photo of a VW Beetle I owned years ago; I kept the picture for nostalgia. I showed it to her and her eyes grew.

"Yeah that's the car, it was orange too," she said and bounced in her chair as if she won a contest.

"Well, thank you, all of you. I have something to go on now." I turned to the sheriff, "I'm done with them, I'm going to call the ME now." I stood and went outside to the front.

I speed dialed Joe Lang, Clark County ME and after a few rings, he answered.

"Joe, this is Jim Richards. I need to ask a really big favor. Are you doing anything today?'

About two hours later, we were in Ash Springs with the sheriff and Mark's body. It was delivered to the sheriff's office and then we took him to the funeral home. Marks' widow, Louise rode along with the sheriff to make the burial arrangements. The funeral director met us at the delivery door and brought out a gurney to take the body in. I parked next to the sheriff's wagon and Buck and I followed everyone in. I was surprised to see Joe Lang sitting at a table with a coffee cup in hand.

"Joe you got here fast," I said with a smile.

"I'm an old friend of Harry here," he pointed to the funeral director, "I haven't seen him in a while so came up right away, I have nothing better to do than look at more dead bodies."

"Well, I thank you for that. I hope I explained everything over the phone that may help your autopsy."

"I get the picture. I read in the paper about the murder, this will be so cool to autopsy someone from area 51."

"Joe, he's not an alien, he's just a worker who got murdered. I'd like your take on it. I'm glad the widow is in the next room so she can't hear us."

Joe went to the cold room of the funeral home and his friend Harry gave him some scrubs. They plotted and planned over the now naked body of Huston. I went to the waiting room where Louise Huston was sitting looking upset.

"I'm sorry about the autopsy, but if it helps catch Mark's killer, it's important," I said.

"It's not the autopsy; it's the cost of the funeral. I used up all our life savings. That is a crime also, the cost of dying." She started to cry, I saw a box of tissues on a table and went to get her one, she thanked me.

I stood watching her for a moment and then excused myself, going out of the room and found Harry. I asked if he had a minute and we went to his office. After a half hour, Harry went back to Louise and gave her the check she used to pay for the funeral arrangements.

"What's this?" she asked.

"Your husband's funeral has been paid for, so take your check back."

"Who?"

"A friend. That's all you need to know." He went back to help Joe Lang, leaving Louise looking confused.

**

Chapter 13

Trapper and Josh Harper went through the back room of Rancid Ricky Collissi's dry cleaning business and loan sharking, and came up with just enough bookkeeping to put Ricky out of business for a while. Trapper was looking for anything that tied into the missing brother or sister, depending on surgery. He checked rooms around the building, looking through files and came up with not one shred of evidence to tie Rickie to Phyllis other than the loan info. Otherwise, he found nothing.

Area 51 Murders

Josh came up behind him as he stood in Ricky's office and said, "Sorry Will, it's a bust for finding your client. Ricky said he knew nothing more about Hathaway. I hate to say it, but I have to believe him. You said that Hathaway was going for a sex change, maybe he's already going through it and is hidden away in some clinic healing."

"Yeah, I thought of that, you know of any good snip and clip places around Vegas?"

"Ouch, no, that stuff usually takes place out in Denver and LA and from what I hear over in Amsterdam. The sister doesn't know about the change?"

"No, I'm going to have to have a heart to heart with her. This is something her brother should tell her, not me. Well, drop me back by my car and I'll let you go process Ricky."

"Yep, this was a good bust; at least we got him out of business for a while until some smart lawyer gets him off."

"Yeah, don't you just hate that?" Trapper laughed as they went out leaving the crime scene men to do their job.

Trapper drove down the strip again and headed to Sam's high-rise. He parked and took the elevator to her floor. She threw open the door with a hopeful look on her face. She could tell by Trapper's scowl that he didn't have good news.

"We need to sit," was all he said.

She went to the couch and waited for Trapper to join her. He went to the wet bar and poured a stiff drink, downed it, then poured another that he took with him to the couch.

"Please don't tell me he's dead."

"Nope, I can't tell you that, I don't know. But I'll tell you what I do know." He took a sip of the drink and then just held on to it. "Sam, how much do you really know about your brother and his job?"

"Actually not much, I'm usually so busy with my life I don't get to include him. Why, is there something I need to know?"

"How do you feel about male to female preferences?"

"Transgendered? I have two trannies working for me in the salon; they're great stylists. They're both pre-op transsexuals and are working for the money to undergo SRS." She studied Trapper face and then said, "Are you saying Phil is transgendered?"

Trapper nodded his head. She sat back and then reached for Trapper's drink from his hand and took it all down in one gulp.

"Good whiskey," She said.

"Yep." Trapper said.

"I knew Phil was a little loose in the shoes, oh God, that is so wrong to say. He had a feminine side I could tell but I didn't know it was this serious. What else do you know?"

"Well I think he wanted to borrow the money from you to pay off a loan shark who was looking for payback. We got the loan shark on ice now but he doesn't know where your brother is. He did say that Phillip, or Phyllis as friends in the Venus Club call her, told him he needed the loan for surgery. I think he's undergoing the change, I don't know where he is or how far into this he's gone. I'm not finished investigating, I just wanted to tell you."

"Thank you. I love my brother and would have helped him if he only confided in me."

"It's hard, I know. I had a friend in Michigan that committed suicide because his family rejected him badly for his crossdressing preference. He came out and they told him to go to hell."

Trapper and Sam were quiet for a while.

~~*~~

The sheriff was standing just past the table where Joe Lang was cutting and probing the body. I came into the room and went to the sheriff. I really couldn't look to the body, I hated blood and guts.

"Jimmy, I can give you a quick appraisal, the COD was a bullet to the back of the head, execution style. But he was tortured first before death. Arms and wrists show marks of being tied and his chest area shows burn marks consistent with electrical shock. Cattle prod, maybe, the marks look right. Looks like they or he also strangled the vic up to just before they allowed him to aspirate his breath. This boy was treated badly. That's my professional opinion."

"Thanks Joe, can you write that all up so I have it for the investigation."

"Glad to oblige. You say you're paying for my trip out here?"

I paused then said cautiously, "Sure, why not. Just don't run up any bills partying."

"Me party? I'm a medical examiner, I live around corpses and death. I have to party to get it out of my system. But I'll go easy on the hookers."

"Thanks Doc, I appreciate that."

"If we don't tell Penny, I'll share a hooker with you." I could tell he was grinning through his mask.

"Are you kidding, she has radar, if I even look at a woman a bell in her head goes off. Thanks but no."

"Your loss, but I'll have something down on paper for you before I leave. Sheriff, do you have any jurisdiction on this murder?"

"It was committed on federal property, I'm out of the loop," the sheriff replied.

"Well, I hope you can catch the perp who did this Jim, this boy suffered before he died."

"Thanks Doc, I'll try my best."

Buck was sitting on a bench outside of the funeral home, reading a paperback book.

"You don't like police stations and funeral homes, anywhere else I should know?" I said.

"Nope that's it. Cops and dead bodies, things I rather avoid. What's the prognosis for our case?"

"Really, prognosis? Are you learning big words now? The Doc says he was tortured before he was murdered, execution style. I'm not going to make a big deal out of it in front of the widow. Bad enough she lost her husband, don't need to make it worse for her."

My cell phone rang and it said private, I answered, it was Harley. "What's up, Harley?"

"I need to see you ASAP when you get back. I don't want to say anything over the phone so look me up. You know where." He hung up.

"That was strange; Harley is hot to tell me something. Shall we head back?" I went in and told everyone that we were heading back to Rachel, Louise looked to me and said thank you quietly. I nodded to her and left the building.

Bob Moats

We arrived back in town and to the A'Le'Inn finding Harley sitting on his usual stool. He grinned and gave me a motion with his hand to follow. We went out to the parking lot and he went to a beefed up Ford pick-up, we followed. He opened the door to the cab and reached under the passenger seat and pulled out a manila envelope and was holding it low, like he didn't want anyone to see it.

"This morning I was cleaning out the beast and found this stuck under the passenger seat. I think Mark left it there to hide. It may have something to do with what Mark was involved in. Take it from me, I don't want anything to do with it."

I took the manila envelope from Harley and thanked him. "Did you look at the contents?"

"I just opened the flap and peeked in, the papers look like something I don't want to be caught with. You decide what to do with it. Maybe this is what Mark was trying to get off the base."

I thanked him again and took Buck back to our room. I closed the door and locked it, taking the package to the bed and dumping the contents out. I sorted through the papers as Buck sat on the end of the bed watching. I read a couple pages and looked up to Buck.

"Wow, this is some hot stuff. I'm not a scientist but what I do read, things here tell me that this is something that has to do with bio warfare. The last page is not the end, it looks like there may be more pages, but they aren't here. This could be why Mark was tortured, for these papers. He didn't give them up."

"You gonna call the Major?" Buck asked.

"No, I think we will hold on to this and use it to our advantage. I'm going to warn Harley not to say a word about it." I put the papers back in the envelope and looked around for a hiding place. I pulled up the area rug in the room over by a corner of the room. I put the envelope under the rug and smoothed it out. Looked good to me.

Buck and I went back to the inn and I warned Harley not to tell anyone about the envelope.

"I may be rough around the edges but I'm not crazy. Envelope, what envelope?" he smiled and went back to his beer.

**

Chapter 14

Buck was sprawled out on the big bed snoring loudly.

I laid on the cot thinking about the implications of what I had read from the papers in the envelope. I was no expert on the subject or even understood what the formulas that I saw could do; I didn't have the rest of the story to know.

Bio warfare, it was not something that should be shared with the world. I couldn't understand the technical terms in the papers, but the heading, "Bio Warfare as it pertained in today's world" was a header I could understand. The paper went on to tell about certain gases and germ agents created by our government that could be released into combat zones to subdue and immobilize enemy combat troops. I wasn't a peace-nick kind of guy, but I didn't approve of what I read. American or foreign, this was wrong.

I had shot and killed a few people in my career as a private investigator, it was necessary, although I would take it personally and occasionally have bad dreams about my killing people, but the mass killing of humans as outlined in the papers was unacceptable. I wondered if I should destroy these papers or use them to my advantage. Destroying them probably would be useless, the government most likely had copies, so that was a wasted effort, but this copy was meant to be sold to outside factions. Terrorist or criminals bent on taking over territories, for the wrong reasons.

The papers went on to diagram the chemical agents and formulas used in the biological processes to make these weapons to take down an army. I couldn't let that happen. Although the papers I had weren't complete, they still carried some weight for making bad stuff to kill many people.

I decided to rest my mind and called Penny before going to sleep. It was almost ten in the evening, but I was sure she would still be up.

"Hey foxy woman, how's life back home?" I said after she answered.

"Lonely without you, but Eric is starting up the B-B-Q and we are going to have steak for our late night meal."

"I'm going to find your Eric one day and murder him. So be aware if he disappears." I laughed.

"You'll never catch him, he's clever," she said with a snicker.

"Don't underestimate my powers."

"So have you caught the aliens yet?"

"We're getting closer; we have new info to take down our bad guy. I'll fill you in when I get back."

"When might that be so I can get all my boyfriends out of the house?"

"You like pushing my buttons, don't you? That's all right; I know you live in a fantasy world so I don't object."

"Fantasy my fanny. I have an active imagination and it manifests itself into real situations and people so I can live out my fantasy. Try that sometime."

"I have already; Pixie is still in my memory banks."

"I told you to get rid of her," she yelled.

"And you were supposed to be rid of Eric, so we're even."

"Okay, Eric for Pixie, that's a fair trade, just as long as they are gone when we are together."

"You got it, sexy woman. Think of me tonight and kiss Willy for me." She said she would and we finished our call.

I put my head on my pillow and smiled at the thought of my wonderful wife.

The next morning Buck was up and farting in the bathroom, I just held my nose and did my morning ritual. I came out and we got ready to go to our first day of working on the base. I was actually a little nervous, but held it well as we went out to go to Fred's home to drive into the base to play act our parts.

"Are you guys ready to start?" Fred asked as we got out of Trapper's Jeep and went to his Ford Bronco.

"Yep as ready as we'll ever be. You'll need to give us the courage to get on the base without falling apart," Buck said as we approached the vehicle.

He explained the procedure for access to the base and we would need to follow closely behind his vehicle to the parking lot where we would be picked up by the base bus. We went back to the Jeep and drove out behind Fred on the long road we had driven on a number of times now to the main gate. We parked in the employee lot, got out, with our toolboxes supplied by Fred, and went to the gate. Fred explained we were new workers and he received our badges from the guard. We clipped them on as we waited for the bus to take us in.

Harley was on the bus with us, after he arrived in his pick-up. He knew better than to blow our cover, he remained quiet about us other than we were new guys on the job. He played the part well.

We pulled into a very large hanger, one for the aircraft that would inhabit the building. We disembarked from the bus and were taken to the area were we would work. We had a couple of guards to watch over us, making sure we didn't do anything unauthorized.

Buck and I went into a room as Fred followed us in. "This is the central point for the wiring of the communications for this hanger. We need to wire up the boxes so they can talk to each other. I'll do most the work, you guys just look like you are doing something, I'll cover for you."

I was watching for someone who fit the description of this Dylan. We spent the next couple of hours pretending to be busy with the wiring that Fred was doing most the work on.

Lunchtime came and we were told to go eat. We went to the picnic table I was told about by Fred and we sat eating our lunches from the pails we brought with us. Buck and I had done a little shopping in Ash Springs before we left, for the necessary equipment we would need to look the part of electrical workers.

We finished and went back to work, to our fake jobs. We went around the entire day trying to look like we knew what we were doing; we had fun actually. The end of the day came and I hadn't seen anyone matching the description of Dylan. I knew I would have to call the Major to fill him in on the info we received.

I was disappointed, but maybe tomorrow he would show up. The bus drove us back to the parking lot and we departed the base.

"Now that was not bad," Buck said, "I may join the electrical workers union."

I looked to Buck and saw he was grinning. "You are so full of it. You do know they take a cut of your pay, right."

"Hmm... I guess I'll have to be a scab worker."

It was now just five-thirty and I took out my cell phone when we got back to the room. I dialed the Major's number and he picked up on the first ring, I liked that.

"Major, it's Jim Richards. I have a lot to tell you and will need some help from your end," I said and then explained to him what we found out about Dylan.

"If you can find out anything about him to help, but keep it on the QT, in case there are others who may be in on this. If you can find out some way to get him to me so I can start my plan for him, I'd appreciate it."

"Mr. Richards, I'll personally pull up his records and find out what he does on the base, I'm sure I can drive him your way. I'll call as soon as I find out." He finished and hung up.

Buck and I went to the inn and ordered dinner. The sheriff came in shortly after and over to us.

"Any luck with your plan?" he asked as he sat.

"It was a bust today, but I called the Major and he is going to see if he can start something going on his end to have Dylan come around so I can pull him in."

"Are you sure Dylan will fall for it?"

"Well, if he wants the other papers we have, he'll have to do something."

"You hope that the papers in your possession are what he needs and he didn't grab off a new copy from the base."

"That is a thought. I'm still wondering why Mark jumped the bus to stay on the base. Was he meeting with Dylan to pull off their plan? Or did he have another reason? Well, time will tell."

My cell phone rang and I answered. It was the Major.

"Mr. Richards, I pulled up Dylan Weeks file on the computer, he is one of the workers in the Biotech department. As you said the papers you have are involving Bio Warfare, correct?"

"I'm not an expert on the subject or even care, but the gist of it was that, yes."

"Well, the papers you have are part of a larger project; the chemical composition that the info creates can wipe out an entire city the size of Las Vegas. You need to keep the papers safe until you can get them back to us. This is no joke now or a simple murder."

Chapter 15

"I'll give you one more day to see if you can find out from Dylan if this is bigger than just a theft of the papers. We need to know if he has outside backing or if he's alone in it. I'm not alerting the Biotech people yet, I want answers from him, not panic from a bunch of scientists. If you can't come up with some answers by tomorrow evening we may have to take him in and do what we can to get the information out of him."

"I'll do my best to get him to talk, how are you going to lead him to me?"

"I'm having you go to him. I've arranged for you, your partner and Fred to go into the Bio lab tomorrow morning under the pretense of adding some communication equipment to the lab. It's going to be installed as a safety feature. Once inside, you will find him and do what you planned. Once you have any statements from him let me know ASAP and we'll take it from there. Good luck and be careful."

I hung up and said to the sheriff and Buck, "This is getting serious, the info I have hidden has information that could wipe out a large city like Las Vegas." I looked to Buck, "The Major is sending us into the Bio lab tomorrow to find Dylan and get any information from him. I hope he still needs our papers."

Area 51 Murders

"The papers you have can't be the only copies of the formula," Buck said.

"I'm sure they aren't, but this copy could be sold to others who want to use it for evil purposes. Once the terrorist have the formula, there's not much the U.S. can do about it."

We finished our meal and the sheriff went off to do what sheriff's do. Buck and I retreated to our room to relax and I attached my laptop to the phone line so I could hookup to the dial-up service I used in emergencies. I spent a little time checking my emails and then explored Google about bio warfare. I went to Wikipedia, where I get most of my information, real or made up. I found a very long article about Biological Warfare, which said that there was a treaty established to ban bio warfare in use, but research can go on as a defensive measure. I'm sure that didn't stop world governments from doing their research into ways of destroying humans.

According to the article many of the substances used included anthrax, tularemia, brucellosis, Q-fever, VEE, botulism and staphylococcal Enterotoxin B was produced as an incapacitating agent. There were a bunch of other chemicals listed but I noticed two that made me wonder, bird flu, and the toxin ricin. Ricin was deadly and would kill, but the article said that to put ricin in use as a weapon, it should be noted that as a biological weapon or chemical weapon, ricin might not be considered very powerful in comparison with other agents such as botulinum or anthrax. Furthermore, the quantity of ricin required to take out a large geographic area is significantly more than an agent such as anthrax. A military willing to use biological weapons and having advanced resources would rather use anthrax instead. The major reason ricin is dangerous is that it is very easy to obtain since it was made from the castor bean plant, which is a common ornamental, and can be grown at home without any special care. That chilled me; anyone could make their own ricin at home.

I was getting weary and wanted to be on my best in the morning so I closed up the laptop and headed to bed. Buck was already out and sawing logs. I went to sleep rather fast, I was worn out.

I was half-asleep as the bus took us to the hanger. There was a deuce and a half truck waiting for us, to take us to the Bio Lab. I had dreams about chemicals being let loose on me and I was suffocating from it. I survived the dream but slept poorly. I had to perk up for my meeting with Dylan Weeks.

We rode in the back of the truck and arrived at the building. We had a guard escort us into the building and then we went through a bunch of checks to make sure we didn't have anything explosive in our toolboxes or on our person.

We were given badges that would register any radiation, since they had isotopes stored here, we were told. The guard handed us off to another guard who took us to a series of sliding doors that seemed to suck in air as they opened. We were pointed to a room that held the communications wiring and told to do our thing.

As we went to the door I saw a man who fit the description of Dylan, he was working at a table with lot of bottles and tubes and equipment that I didn't understand.

Area 51 Murders

Fred set us up with the props that we would use to fake our attempts to hook up an alarm system for the lab. They already had one but our cover was to install a back up. As time went on everyone ignored us, so I started to wander around carrying a long length of wire. I came up to Dylan as he moved closer to me and I whispered, "Dylan."

He looked surprised and turned to me, "Are you talking to me?"

"Is there any other Dylan Weeks in here, slick?"

"Who are you?" he asked cautiously.

"I'm the guy replacing Mark Huston. I got the package," I said not knowing if it was correct, hoping I was saying the right thing. He gave me a shocked look and turned to see where the other workers were, then turned back to me.

"How did you get it?"

I had no idea, so just played it up. "Mark passed it to me, but he got killed, you know anything about that?" I went to put him on the defensive.

"Hey that wasn't me. I didn't want him killed, but he wouldn't give up the location of the file or the bomb. Do you have the bomb too?"

My heart dropped a bit wondering what the hell was the bomb. "No, Mark never mentioned it, just the papers. What is the plan now?"

He gave me a strange look; I was worrying that I may have said something wrong. He continued, "I thought you people would have the plan. Mark was changing the set it up, but Howie didn't like the deal and put Mark through the ringer to tell him where the stuff was. You don't know?"

"I got everything second hand from Mark; he only gave me enough because he was in a hurry to get the plan working. Why did he stay the night on the base?"

"We found out that Mark took the parts for the bomb and hid them, we thought he put them in his car, we tried to check it. The military police was getting nosy about why we were searching the car. We made excuses of looking for a missing cell phone; they stopped us before we could finish. The car wasn't supposed to be in the lot after hours. They questioned us and we made up the same excuse about the cell phone. I hope the bomb parts weren't in the car. They brought it in after they found Mark. Stupid Howie left him lying out in the open."

I took a stab, "Mark never mentioned someone named Howie."

"He's the man in charge of manifests for most of the cargo planes on the base, he was setting up the shipment of the bomb off the base to use it, but Mark got to it first. Howie was furious that he got the parts."

"What's Howie's plan now?"

"He hasn't said; I haven't seen him since yesterday early. I don't even know what to do now."

I stood looking at him; he wasn't very smart acting, a little vague in the head. "What were you going to do with the papers and this bomb if you had it?"

"Howie was going to make all of us tons of money, now we may not see a penny. Where do you have the other part of the papers?"

"I have them hidden, where they will stay till I meet this   Howie."

"That's something you may not want. He may kill you too if you don't give up the papers."

"So what's a cargo jockey doing hustling bio weapons?"

"We're friends and I talk too much. He has connections overseas through the cargo planes; he knows the right people and had me set the theft up. Mark was willing to take the stuff off the base in his car, but things went wrong when we found that Mark had taken the parts to assemble the bomb. Howie got hold of him and in one of the empty hangers, he tortured him to find out what he did with it. Howie couldn't make him talk and got mad. He stupidly killed him. But this is good; you have the papers at least."

"Can't you smuggle out more parts for the bomb?"

"Are you kidding, I had to fudge inventory to cover the ones we took. Anymore and it would be discovered."

"So if you had this bomb what was Howie going to do with it?"

"Oh, it was going to be great, Howie was going to take it up in one of his planes, up high in the sky, it's an airborne chemical virus, and release it."

"Release it where?"

"Las Vegas of course, it'll wipe everybody out."

**

Chapter 16

Las Vegas was sunny and hot as people went about their daily chores and activities, gambling, taking in shows and totally uncaring about the rest of the world in the moment. Trapper was escorting Sam to his car; they were going to the Venus Club to see if they could track Phyllis from there.

He drove out as Sam sat quietly in her seat. "Do you have an opinion on what I told you about your brother?" Trapper asked.

"Yes, but it's personal," she said as she watched out the car window at the people on the strip going about not thinking on the subject of missing people or gender issues. Why don't they care she wondered to herself. She let out a big sigh and finally spoke, "The world is not nice, Will. There is so much hate and bigotry out there it makes the rest of us who do care, wary about being open. It makes those who are different afraid of what others think. I see it at the salon, from the two pre-op transsexuals that work there. They are both convincing as women, but every now and then, someone spots the difference, they start their shit about not wanting the queer guys working on them. Damn people, how many jokes are told about gays working in the hair business? Besides, they aren't gay, they are gender dysphoric, they live in the wrong bodies. A cruel fate given to them by biology and God. If there is a God. Does God make mistakes? How can all these Christians call themselves that when they rally against other human beings? Take that fine group of churchgoers who protested at a soldier's funeral just because he was gay. Stupid asses."

Trapper quietly watched the road and waited for her to let it out.

"When Phillip was young, he was a bit feminine. Our father hated it and was rough on him, treating him like a pariah. I felt so sorry for him but didn't stand up for him. I was one of those who are afraid of what others think about us. Stupid, stupid, stupid." Trapper could see a tear roll down her cheek, he pulled out his handkerchief and gave it to her.

"As I said I had friends back in Michigan who had the same lifestyle. They would talk to me about it. I know there is a stigma on being different; it's hard to let the world know unless you are ready to fight for it. Shame there has to be a fight to be what you want to be," Trapper said as they pulled into the Venus Club parking.

Bob Moats

Trapper used the valet parking and took Sam into the club. It was not very busy, being that it was still early in the day. Tammy AKA Tommy, was at the bar, saw Trapper and waved. Trapper guided Sam to two empty stools and they sat.

"Hey cutie, you came back. And who is this luscious lady with you?" Tammy asked.

"Tammy, this is Sam, Phyllis' sister. Sam this is Tammy."

Tammy held out her hand and they shook, "Pleasure to meet the sister of our favorite girl. I just hope she comes back to work, I'm tired of overtime." Tammy laughed at her comment and continued, "Have you located her yet?"

"Nope but I did find the thugs who were bothering her. They won't be coming around for a while. Did you know that Phyllis wanted a sex change?"

"Hell, babe, all of us here want a sex change, but it's just expensive and a really big commitment. You have to be in the right place in your life to actually do it. Although I think Phyllis would be there, she talked a lot about it, enough to do it."

"If one were to get the change, where might one go?"

"Out of town, probably the Baxter Clinic in LA, there's no real place to do it here. At least none that are good at it."

Area 51 Murders

"If Phyllis wasn't worried about the quality of the work, where in town could that operation be performed?"

"You think she's in one of the cutting mills? I hope she isn't, the surgery they perform is below par, I knew a girl who went to one and almost died from complications. Hold on." Tammy went to a book on the back bar and thumbed through it, and then wrote something on a napkin bringing it back to Trapper.

"Here's the address of the clinic, if she's there, I just hope you find her in good condition, and alive."

~~*~~

"Set loose a bio virus over Las Vegas? Are you nuts, there are women and children there, even so, you can't kill all those people!" I spoke louder, causing others in the room look over to us. I waved and apologized for the outburst. They were wrapped up in their work enough to ignore us or understand what I had said. Luckily, our guard was busy talking to some blond by the entrance and ignoring us.

I looked back to Dylan and gave him a glare. He finally spoke, "What? I don't care and Howie hates the city. He grew up there; he wasn't a very popular person. He wants to make an example of the potency of the bomb to show our potential investors that it has the power to do what we say. He takes care of two things, destroy the city and impress the world. He's crazy you know. I said you have to avoid him."

"Yeah, well I'm not in on this destruction. If Howie wants the rest of the equipment to pull off his plan, he will have to deal with me now. I think I know where Mark hid the bomb. Make a meeting happen and we can discuss it."

"I'll call him and see if he is willing to meet. Where?"

"At the A'Le'Inn over in Rachel, in room three. Tonight, at eight and we'll talk then." I turned to go back into the room where Buck and Fred were standing around killing time talking.

"We need to get out of here," I said and started to gather the tools I brought in. Fred asked if I made contact with Dylan and what I had found out.

"I need to get back to the Major on this, we don't have a lot of time. I need to talk to Harley first though, let's go back to the hanger."

We were taken back to the hanger where Harley was stringing up power lines. I called him down from the scaffolding he was up on. He climbed down and we went off to the side of the building.

"Harley, when you found the envelope in your truck did you do a thorough cleaning? I mean everywhere in the truck?"

"I did a quick clean up for a date I had so I just managed the cab and the truck bed."

"Do you think Mark could have put a package in your truck? I don't know how big a package it would have been but it may be in your truck."

"Yeah, he could have, there are places on my truck a package could be hidden. You think he had something else planted?"

"I'm hoping he did. We need to check after we get out of here. I'll ride with you and we'll stop outside of the base property to check, is that all right?"

"Yeah, sure, okay by me." He looked at his watch and said we had an hour before quitting time and we can go.

I didn't have my cell phone because we were warned not to bring them on the base with us. I went to Fred and asked if there was some way to call the Major from the hanger. He went to his toolbox and pulled out a technician's clip phone and then he went to the junction box for the phone system. He clipped the leads to the wires in the box and handed me the handset. "Dial your number and the call should go through," he said.

I dialed the Major's number and two rings later, he answered. He was slowing down I thought. "Major, it's Jim, I got some info for you and it's scary." I told him about what Dylan had told me and I said I was going to be trying to locate the bomb parts and would let him know what I find. I just didn't tell him where I thought they were, possibly in Harley's truck. I told him I had a couple places to look, but nothing definite.

"Mr. Richards, find those parts, this is not just a theft, it could be mass murder. I'm going to have some men go pick up Dylan and this Howie, I'll look him up. Thank you Mr. Richards, and we owe you a debt of gratitude."

"Please keep me informed about what you find out. Thanks." We finished and I hung up giving the handset back to Fred. He was standing by listening.

"Are you saying there is bomb capable of wiping out all of Las Vegas?"

"We won't really know until they use it, but hopefully I can find it before they can carry out the deed."

Buck said, "Can I go back and pound on Dylan for a while?"

"No Buck, you can't, but I think the Air Force will do that. The Major is sending men to take Dylan and his partner. Hopefully it will stall their plans for this."

About ten minutes later five big military policemen went into the Bio Lab led by Captain D'Amico. They stormed up to Dylan.

"Dylan Weeks, you are under arrest for terrorist activities against the United States. Get him out of here."

**

Chapter 17

I arranged with the Major to meet Captain D'Amico at the main gate to give him the SD card from my pocket recorder. I had used it while I talked to Dylan so we'd have proof of what he said. I had to smuggle the recorder on the base, they didn't like recorders in top secret areas, but the Major said they'd over look my breaking the rules. I could tell he was smiling when he said it.

At the main gate we met with the Captain, he told me that they had Dylan under custody but they couldn't find Howard Hulland, the cargo jockey. He left the base earlier, just after Dylan called him when Buck, Fred and I left the Bio Lab. I was disappointed, and worried, Howie was still loose and dangerous.

"Mr. Richards, if you can keep us abreast of the bomb's location, it would be helpful and you can call me as soon as possible." He handed me his card and turned on his heels going back to the jeep that hauled him out here. I turned to my crew and asked Harley if we could depart the area so we could search the truck.

Buck took Trapper's Jeep and followed us about five miles from the base to a secluded area off the road. "Okay let's go on a hunt for a bomb." Harley gave me a panicked look, "Don't worry it's not active," I said to reassure him, but I wasn't so sure if it was dangerous yet.

Buck pulled up behind us and walked to Harley's truck as he and I were digging around the cab. Buck went down on the ground and was under the truck for a few minutes. I would pause in my search to watch him doing something down there. He scooted out and in his hand was what looked like a box wrapped in newspaper.

"It's a place I used to hide my stash back when I indulged in pot. I figured he might have put it there, I was right," he said with a puffed up chest. I gave him a pat on the back and told him I would give him a bonus.

"Sure, you aren't charging the widow for this adventure, so you're going to pay me out of your pocket. Right?"

"I'll owe you."

"I'll put it with all the other 'I'll owe yous'."

I decided to wait on opening the wrapping for when we got back to the room. I would put the papers I had with the box and take them to the Major in the morning.

"Thanks Harley and this is not to be mentioned to anyone until I get this back to the proper authorities. It's dangerously hot." He agreed, got in his truck and then drove off.

I stood on the shoulder of the road looking out to the miles of barren desert land and thinking this could be what Las Vegas could look like if this box where in the wrong hands. I turned to Buck, "Shall we leave this hell hole?"

He grinned and got behind the wheel as I carefully took the box and put it on my lap. We drove back in silence and into the parking lot of the inn, where I quickly took the box to the room, hoping to avoid anyone seeing me.

"This is getting to be a very black ops kind of thing isn't it?" Buck asked.

I flashed on our real black ops agent, former agent, Earl Daws and would have to tell him about this when I saw him. "I'll bet Earl never handled a Bio weapon before while he was saving the country from evil," I said with a smile.

I looked around the room for a place to put the box and saw the ceiling tiles above. I pulled a chair over and stood up on it where I pushed the ceiling panel aside and placed the box overhead and pulled the panel back in place.

"I thought you wanted to open the thing?"

"I'm not interested in setting the thing off, it may be booby trapped. I pulled off this paper taped to the box, hopefully it will explain things." I put the chair back and sat on it as I unfolded the paper, then reading it aloud to Buck.

"It says, 'If you're reading this I'm probably dead. Harley, it you find this box don't open it, it is dangerous and you need to take it to the police and show this letter to them. This box contains three vials of chemicals that if combined would turn into an airborne virus that would expand exponentially into a cloud of gas that has the capability to kill all living beings for a hundred square miles. Howie Hulland, base cargo officer and his partner Dylan Weeks from the Bio Lab, plotted to sell the plans of creating the chemicals to the highest bidder from a network of terrorist from around the world. Howie had planned to combine the chemicals over the city of Las Vegas to prove the formula works. All citizens of Vegas would die horribly leaving nothing but a pile of rotting carcasses. I can't let this happen. If I come up dead, take this to the authorities immediately. Thanks Harley, you've been a good friend, Mark'. That's it," I said. "I guess he had noble intentions, I'll be sure to let his wife and son know that he died saving the world."

We went into the inn for dinner before resting for the night. On cue the sheriff came in and over to us. "Anything new?" he said as he sat.

"We caught the killer and his accomplice, but the feds only have the accomplice, the killer is still on the loose, so be on the watch for him," I said.

"What's he look like?"

"Didn't the Major send out a picture of the guy to all the law enforcement agencies?"

"I haven't been in the office today; I'll call to see if they got something. You find the thing that everyone is looking for?"

"Nope, I'm still looking. But as soon as I find it, everyone will know."

"Works for me, are you going to tell Louise about the killer?"

"I'm not looking to do that but she needs to know we identified him. You're a friend of hers; could you go with me to talk to her?"

"Sure it's the least I can do; I don't feel like I'm doing enough about this, my hands have been tied. When do you want to go?"

I looked to Buck, he had finished his meal, I wasn't hungry anymore, "Now works for me."

"Okay, I'll follow you out, just don't speed, I haven't gotten my quota of tickets today." He laughed, stood and went out the front door.

Buck asked, "Why didn't you tell him you did find the bomb?"

"I'm not telling anyone about it, I'd feel safer if no one knew we had it."

"Smart, that way we don't end up dead too."

"Yep, shall we go?"

We drove out to Louise's trailer and she opened the door as we approached. She gave me a hopeful look and I asked her to sit inside. We went into the trailer, Mitch was nowhere to be seen, Louise could see I was looking for the boy.

"Mitchell is out back in his tree house. He's still not over his father being gone. Do you have any word for me, Mr. Richards?"

"We have identified the murderer, he was an officer on the base who had plotted to sell secrets to terrorists, but your husband did what he could to stop them. Unfortunately, it cost him his life. The military investigations department has one man in custody but the man who committed the crime is still being sought. It will only be a matter of time before they catch him."

"Louise, on my way here I called my office and we now have the photo of the killer, I have every available man in the Sheriff's Department out looking for him, we'll catch him," the sheriff said quietly.

"Thank you, everyone who helped. I won't sleep well, but a little better knowing he has been identified. Please let me know as soon as they find him. I'd like to face him and tell him how he left my son broken hearted." She started to tear up and took a tissue from a box that looked like it was well used.

"Wait here please, I'd like you to tell my son how his father tried to stop the bad guys. I think it may help him to get a little closure that his father didn't die for nothing." She stood, went to the back door and out. We waited for about three minutes then I heard a muffled cry from the back. I signaled Buck to follow, the sheriff came up behind us and we went out the back door to the only tree in the yard where Louise was standing below the rough tree house holding a paper in her hand. She had a look of terror on her face and handed me the paper saying she found it tacked to the tree.

I quickly read the paper written in a crude handwriting, but I understood the implications. I read aloud, "You need to get yourselves together and bring me

121

the box and the papers, I know you have them. Don't screw with me, I have the boy and I will not hesitate to cut him into little pieces until you return my property. Get it all together; I will contact you at eight o'clock in your room number three. Be there with the package and NO police or military or the boy dies."

**

Chapter 18

The sheriff was having a fit as I tried to calm Louise. "Sheriff, we need to play this carefully. He seems to know what's going on, he either has a spy or is very good at guessing. Either way I need to face him alone, well, I'll have Buck nearby. If he sees you then Mitch will be in danger, you know that. So please back off for now. I'll keep in touch with you by cell phone when something happens. I need to speak to you alone." I took his arm and pulled him away from Buck and Louise.

"Sheriff, I do have the package that he needs, I didn't mention it before because the less people know the better."

"No problem, I can relate to the caution."

"Here's the thing, he says in the note that he knows I have the package, the only person who knew I did have it is Harley. It was hidden on his truck, he didn't know it was, but he was there when Buck found it under his truck.

I'm sure you know Harley well enough, but I'd suggest watching him."

"I can't believe that Harley would be part of this, but we don't really know people do we?"

"No we don't, so please check him out and stay away from the inn so I can get Mitch back safely. That's my first priority. We've got only two hours before he contacts me, I have to get my mind ready for this. I'll call the Major after I meet with Hulland, I don't want the military roaring in before we have Mitch back safely." I looked around, "There wasn't a lot of places he could have grabbed Mitch and taken him to. This is mostly desert and I don't see any tracks back here, he had to grab the boy and carry him to a car or van off the road. Maybe you can put up road blocks to check vehicles driving out from town."

"I'll call it in and get that taken care of. I need to be part of this, let me take care of that."

"I'm sure Hulland will put the boy somewhere to be in control. He won't give us his location unless he has the package. I hate to say it, but these crimes usually don't end well. I don't want Louise to lose both her husband and her son in the same week."

"Good point, let's just play it by ear and do our best."

"Thanks Sheriff, you need to make a call and take care of Louise. Best if you hung out here to watch her and you'll be close enough if I need you.'

"Okay, what are you going to do now?"

Area 51 Murders

"I'm going to the inn and wait. I hate that but not much else to go on here. So let's just hope everything goes smoothly."

We went back to Louise and Buck, I told Buck we need to go back to the inn. The sheriff stayed with Louise and I drove the Jeep back.

"What do you have planned now?" Buck asked on the road to the inn.

"I have no idea, I don't like this. I've had adults taken to be used as a pawn, but not a child. This makes it worse. I don't want anything to mess this up, so we play it careful."

We pulled into the inn parking and got out of the vehicle. I stood by the Jeep looking around wondering if he may be nearby watching. The whole area was spread out and sparse, so it would be hard to hide somewhere. I didn't see anything out of the ordinary, so we went to the room.

I got up on the chair again and brought down the box, placing it on the writing table. I pulled the chair back to the desk and sat studying the box.

"Are you going to open it?" Buck asked.

I started to carefully peel the newspaper at the side where it was taped. I could see a brown cardboard box under the paper and pulled the remains of the paper off it. I carefully slid the top flap of the box open and looked inside. I found bubble wrap surrounding three glass vials.

I took the vials out hoping I wasn't releasing some dangerous virus into the room, but they looked secure.

"I was told that these three chemicals when combined can create an airborne virus that will kill all people who breathe it. Amazing how such small things can be so deadly. I need some packing tape, can you go to the inn and see if we can borrow some?" Buck said he'd be right back and left the room. I put two of the vials back into the bubble wrap and placed them back in the box. I took the third one and put it safely in my laptop case.

Buck came back a few minutes later and handed me the tape. I pulled off a length of tape and wrapped it around the closed box. "I hope this will delay him long enough to get some info out of him as to what he is doing with Mitch."

I took the box, pulled out the manila envelope of papers from its hiding place and put both of them on the bed. I stood looking at the package that could murder millions of people worldwide if it got into the hands of terrorists.

"All we can do now is wait," I said.

We sat and waited to see what Howie was going to do to get his package. My cell phone rang and it was the sheriff. I said, "I have nothing to tell you, he hasn't showed up yet. How's Louise holding up?"

"Not well, but that's to be expected. I have roadblocks about a half mile outside both ends of town. At least there is only two ways to get into town. Nothing yet from either place. Keep me in the loop," he said then we disconnected.

Another twenty minutes passed, almost eight o'clock when I heard an engine roar coming closer to our building. I went to the back window looking out to the desert and saw it. A small single engine Cessna airplane was landing in the desert behind our building. It came to a rest and I saw a man get out. Just then, there was a knock at our door and I opened it to find the young waitress standing there.

"We got a call at the inn requesting you to go out back to a plane that is landing there and to bring the package. That's all he said." She smiled and went off.

I turned to Buck and told him to watch from the window and if I looked back to him, he was to come running. I picked up the box and papers, put them in a plastic bag from our shopping yesterday, tucked my Glock in my belt behind me and went out of the room. Buck went back to the window and watched.

I slowly approached the plane; it was still running. The man was big and burley, dressed in coveralls and he looked to be about fifty-something, grey hair and ugly. He had a very nasty looking assault rifle in one hand, holding it low. As I got closer and I could see the head of a person in the back seat of the plane, I hoped it would be Mitch. There was another head in the front seat behind where Howie was standing; I couldn't see who it was.

"That's close enough," the man yelled. He motioned to the other person in front and the man got out of the plane coming around towards me. I realized it was Fred.

As he reached me I said, "Fuck you Fred, I thought you were a good guy."

"Hey I got greedy and you got the package. Now give it to me."

I just held my ground. I yelled to Howie, "I want the boy or the papers go up in the wind." I held them up ready to let them spread out in the breeze.

Howie raised the assault rifle and yelled, "Not if you want the boy in one piece. Give the package to Fred, Now!" he barked.

I didn't have much choice, I took the papers and the box and held them out, Fred came up and took them. He ran back to the passenger side of the plane and got in. Howie yelled, "You better hope everything is there."

"I yelled, "Give me the boy!"

"In due time, I need a hostage to be sure I get to where I'm going. Sorry if I lied." He climbed into the plane, I thought about firing my Glock but I didn't want to endanger the boy.

The plane revved up and taxied out to the desert. I stood there helpless. Buck came running up beside me. "You had no choice, Jim."

I pulled my cell phone and called the Major, explaining everything from finding the box in the truck to Howie's flying away in the plane. I told him the make and the numbers I read off the plane and the direction it was heading, South. He wasn't happy that I hadn't called sooner but I defended my reason for the safety of the boy. He still wasn't happy but accepted it. He said he would have someone track the plane and send out a recon plane to follow. He hung up. I felt miserable, I didn't get Mitch and I lost the package.

**

Chapter 19

Major Rickson called me back about a half hour later. "Richards, we sent one of our stealth planes out after we got a radar fix on the thing. It's heading for Vegas. I'd order it to be shot down but I don't want to be responsible for killing a child or setting off the chemicals, so the stealth is tracking it and we will have a fix on where it lands. I have been in touch with Nellis Air Base and they will have men converge on the plane when we have a location. We will resolve this one way or another." He finished and hung up.

I called the sheriff and filled him in on what happened.

"Crap, Howie is flying to Las Vegas," I told Buck. "I don't think he'll try to use the bomb now, he needs to get word out that he's going to perform a huge feat of power, and then he will follow up on it. I'm sure he will be a little pissed to find he doesn't have all the parts of the bomb, I hadn't counted on the boy being taken with them. I hope

Howie doesn't hurt him because of it. I didn't mention to the Major that I had the third vial, I'll probably get in trouble for it, but I need it to make a swap for the boy if it comes down to it. As far as I'm concerned, we're done here, let's get back to Vegas and see what we can do there to stop this nutjob."

Buck smiled and said, "Sounds good, this place is a little too primitive for me." We packed and put the bags in the Jeep. I went to the inn to settle the bill and thanked everyone. Harley wasn't on his stool, I wondered where he was. Buck and I got in Trapper's Jeep, drove by Louise's trailer, and stopped. I told Buck to wait and got out.

I went to the door as Louise came out, followed by the sheriff and Harley. "I'm going back to Vegas where the plane is heading for, the military is tracking it and hopefully they will stop them when they arrive in Vegas. I'll do everything I can to see that Mitch is returned to you, but please don't expect miracles." I didn't want to blow her bubble, but I had to get her braced for it.

She thanked me and I shook the sheriff's hand and said, "It's been a pleasure Sheriff, I hope if you ever get to Vegas, please look me up." I thanked Harley for his help, went back to the Jeep and we left.

It was now just before ten o'clock at night and we drove back in the dark of the desert highway. After about an hour of travel we saw the bright lights of the city ahead, a welcome sight I was glad to see. We went by the office to get our own cars and saw the lights were on in the building. We went in the back door and found Trapper and Sam sitting in his office.

"Hey, you're back. Did you see any aliens?" Trapper asked.

"Nope, just mass killers who may wipe out Vegas," I said and then sat explaining our trip. "So, be prepared to evacuate the city if I call."

"Wow, this is serious. I hope the military can catch them."

"I'm going to be doing my best to help. I'm calling Lynn and Deacon to fill them in also. I need to get the boy back to his mother."

I stood and said, "I'll keep you informed. I have a lot of work to do now." I left them and Buck had already gone to his office to call Mac to see how his guards were doing. He was on the phone when I came by and went to my office. I sat and picked up the phone and called Penny.

"Hi Sweetie, are you still chasing aliens?" she said when she answered up the phone.

"No, I'm back in town, at the office. I don't have a lot of time to explain now, I'll fill you in later. I have more calls to make and I'll be home shortly. Have a couple of cold beers waiting for me, I'm going to need them."

"Sounds serious, I'll be waiting," she said as we finished and I called Lynn at home.

"Hey Fearless, what's up?" she said when she answered.

"I have a long story to tell you, put me on speaker and call Deacon in." She called him and said she was on speaker. I told them about the whole mess and about Hulland flying back to Vegas. "He would have to be around here by now, it should have only taken a short time to fly in. I haven't heard from the Major, I'll call if he doesn't, just to find out if Hulland landed and where. I'll let you guys know and Lynn, since you just got back from training at the FBI Academy in terrorism, you can lend a local authority to it."

"I'll call the Captain about this, even if it is eleven at night, crime never takes a rest. I hope we can catch him and get the boy back safely. Let me know what you hear."

We hung up and I sat back thinking about my next move. Hulland couldn't set off the bomb without my vial, so the city would be safe, I was just worrying about Mitch for now. I was really tired, but made a call to the Major.

"Richards, I was just going to call you. Hulland's plane landed just outside Vegas, Nellis sent a team there by Apache helicopters but he had fled the area. When you get back to Vegas let me know so I can get your perspective on what the hell is going on out there."

"Major, I'm already back in Vegas and ready to help. Did the troops find anything at the plane site that may tell me where to start?"

"No, but I gave you clearance to investigate. You're one person who may get better results from the local authorities to help track Hulland."

"Can you get me any background info on Hulland, I was told he grew up here, he may have some people or places he may go to. I've already called my friends in the Las Vegas PD and they are prepared to help."

"Excellent, I'll get the info and if you give me your email address, I'll forward it to you. I'm sure we have some time before he does something foolish, but we can't delay."

I agreed and gave him my address and said I'd watch for the info. We disconnected and I gathered my things to go home. I said good-bye to Buck and then went in to do the same for Trapper.

"I meant to ask if you found the missing brother."

"I'm still working on it."

I turned to Sam and said, "Don't worry, if anyone can find him, Will can do it." She thanked me for my concern and I said I was leaving and went to my car.

I drove out going through the city, it's light flashing and enticing, I hated to think anything would ever spoil it, I wasn't going to let that happen. I made one stop at a drugstore before going home and found what I needed and headed out. I pulled into the drive, probably setting off the alarms so Penny would know I was home. I headed into the garage and hit the remote to close the door, just as the garage light went on and the inner door to the house opened. Penny opened the door and out flew Willy, coming to bounce at my feet. I picked him up and snuggled him, he was licking my face as if I had sugar on it. I usually didn't like doggy kisses, but I missed him.

"About time you got home, we've been lonely without you," Penny said as she gave me hugs and kisses also.

"Sure, you and Willy probably sat around playing cribbage while I was gone."

"Nope Crazy Eights, and Willy cheats," she said with a hearty laugh, I loved her laugh.

We went in and to the living room where she had a snack table set up with chips and two beers in can coolers. I plopped down on the couch and pulled her to me, giving her big wet kisses, then sat her back. "I have a lot to tell you, so after I take a swig of beer, I'll start."

I sat back and took the can of beer to my lips realizing I hadn't had beer in almost three days, I didn't miss it, but it tasted good. I was quiet for a moment, organizing my thoughts, Penny waited for me. I told her about our trip out and all about the A'Le'Inn and our room. I detailed my visit with Louise and meeting the sheriff. Then I spun the story of how we were involved with the base and Area 51, seeing no aliens, but terrorists. I did mention that I paid for Mark's funeral; Penny just gave me a smile and didn't comment on my spending. I told about Hulland kidnapping Mitch and forcing me to give him the package and I told her that I held back part of the bomb. She asked if it was safe, I said I had it put away where it won't hurt anyone.

About a half hour later, I finished. Penny was amazed by my tale and said so. "Do you think Hulland will harm the boy?"

"If he wants the rest of the chemicals he won't but he may hurt him till he gets what he needs. I hope I can convince him I will only give him the vial in exchange for the boy." I put my head back on the couch as Penny was stroking my head. I fell asleep.

**

Chapter 20

The next morning, Trapper entered the clinic followed at a distance by Sam. She lingered to get her strength together if her brother was in this building changing his sex. She still wasn't sure how she would react to the situation. She grew up loving her brother, but she hadn't been there for him enough. Now she had to get used to a whole new person, a sister she just discovered.

Trapper went to the reception counter and showed the girl his P.I. badge and ID, which she studied closely. He put it away and asked to see the person in charge.

"That would be Dr. Fleishman, he's in surgery right now.'

"Is he with Phillip AKA Phyllis Hathaway having a sex change?"

"I'm sorry but I can't give out that information, you'll have to wait for the doctor to finish. Or get a warrant."

She turned away leaving Trapper alone. Sam came up behind him.

"Is he here?"

"I don't know yet, she's claiming privilege." He watched the girl go into what looked like a filing room. Then he reached over the counter and picked up an appointment book on the desk. He turned it and ran his finger down the list of patients, reading quickly. He didn't see the name and put the book back before the girl returned.

She re-entered the room. "Did you find what you were looking for?" Then she pointed to a camera in the corner of the ceiling. Trapper smiled and said, "Busted."

The girl smiled back and said she wouldn't tell. Sam moved closer to the counter, "It's my brother, I'm trying to find him, can you tell me anything?"

"Sometimes people come in using aliases, but I still can't tell you anything. We do have two sex changes in but that's all I can say. Maybe your sister was a cute blond? But I can't tell you if we have her here."

"Gee, what can you tell us?" Trapper grinned.

"Oh, I can't say," she said and went back to the file room.

Sam looked to Trapper, "Phil is blond, could it be?"

"I can't say," he smiled, "Let's wait and see."

Area 51 Murders

They sat until Dr. Fleishman came out from somewhere in the back. He hadn't changed out of his scrubs and was messy with blood. Trapper could hear Sam gasp and he stood quickly going to the counter.

"Excuse me, Doc," Trapper said as he flashed his badge briefly so the doctor didn't get a good look. "I'm here looking for a missing person, one Phillip Hathaway. This is his sister and she is worried about him as he has not contacted her that he or she was going for a sex change. We just need to know if this person is safe and here."

The doctor stood staring at Trapper, "Sir I don't have to give out any information about my clients. Get a warrant and I'll tell you." He turned and went back to the place he came from.

The receptionist was standing by the door to the file room; she came forward and put two files on the counter. "Now don't open these and look at the pictures in them. Don't do that." She went back into the file room as Trapper opened the files, pulling the before pictures out and showing them to Sam. She let out a breath and said, "Neither of these people are Phil."

Trapper put everything back the way he found it and closed the folders. He called to the girl, "Thank you." She came to the door, smiled and said, "Sorry I couldn't help."

Trapper and Sam went back to his Jeep that was returned to him last night and they sat for a short while, not speaking. Sam's cell phone rang and she looked at the ID, it said private. "Hello?"

She heard a barely audible, shaky voice, "Sam, it's me, help me." Then the call ended.

~~*~~

I woke refreshed but anxious, I had slept well, but had dreams I didn't like. Between aliens and terrorist and watching the city of Las Vegas melt in a puddle of goo, I didn't want to sleep again.

Penny was getting ready to go to her show, it was early morning now, and my visit to Area 51 was one I wouldn't forget in a long while. "I can call in sick, and spend the day with you. I don't want the world to blow up and be separate from you," she said.

I smiled and kissed her nose, "No babe, the world won't end today, but I'll let you know when. I'll make sure we are together for the rest of our lives."

She left for work and I finished dressing when my phone rang, it was the Major. "Hello."

"Richards, I sent the file on Hulland, you should have it now. Have you found out anything on your end?"

"No, I'm just now getting organized. I have to call my friends in LVMPD again to set up a meeting with their team, led by the local FBI trained terrorist expert, I'll take the files you sent and we will work the case from here. I'll be sure you are kept informed."

Area 51 Murders

"Thank you, I've contacted a Captain Goodson, he's out of Nellis and he is the military liaison for our Special Investigation Division and he will contact you. Keep me in the loop." He hung up.

I went to the computer in my home office and brought up the file in the email. I printed out the pages, put them in a manila envelope and put them in my laptop case by the vial I still had in there. I had one project to do before I left so I went out to my workshop in the end of the garage and spent a few minutes working.

I had everything ready and called Lynn. "Good morning, Lieutenant. Are you ready to chase evil people?"

I arrived at Metro PD and parked. I found Deacon, Lynn and the Captain in Lynn's office. I was surprised to see the Captain, he could see my look and said, "Jim, this is serious, I need to be part of this. I grew up in Vegas and I don't want some bastard destroying it."

"Well, welcome Captain. Shall we make some plans?"

We sat talking and looking over the file of Hulland and he had priors for various petty crimes around Vegas. The Captain called to get his rap sheet and we laid out a plan of attack on places he may frequent. The Captain put a priority on this and would send most of his officers out looking for Hulland.

"My main concern is the return of Mitchell Huston, safely, so I hope your men don't act like cowboys and injure the boy," I said.

"I'll warn the men to watch out for the boy, but if Hulland gets shot in the way, well, so be it." The Captain smiled and excused himself. He went out leaving Lynn, Deacon and me alone.

"Okay now that he's gone we can start our investigation." Lynn laughed as she checked again to be sure the Captain was out of earshot.

I was reading the file from the Major; I noticed Hulland's only sibling, a sister, lived in Henderson. I said, "We could start by visiting her," I said as I pointed out the reference in the file. Lynn looked at it and said it was a place to start.

We all got up and went to our cars, I followed Deacon driving Lynn and we went down to Henderson and found the home off the Valley View Parkway. I let them take the lead just in case Hulland was in the house. It was a nice colonial, desert landscaping and looking vacant. There were no curtains in the windows and as we looked in there was no furniture. I found a note posted on the door, it was a foreclosure notice.

"Damn economy, now our suspects are being forced out," I said.

I saw a smaller note taped to the inside of the front door window, it was directions to a place where the family moved to, directions for who I wondered? If it was for Hulland, he may have seen it already. I told Lynn my thoughts, she agreed and we left to follow the directions.

Area 51 Murders

We arrived up in North Vegas by the downtown area, just off Third Street. The house was on a street that looked run down and dingy. The part of town that isn't in the travel brochures. Lynn said she called North Vegas Police Captain Sustaine earlier and explained the terror threat. He said he'd have his men watch for Hulland. They pulled an old photo off his rap sheet and circulated it.

Deacon approached the door with his hand on his service revolver. He knocked and after a few minutes, we could hear movement in the house. The door opened and a woman in her early sixties stood looking at us.

"Yes, can I help you?"

"Mrs. Willington?"

"Yes."

"I'm Detective DeAngelo, this is Lieutenant Carter and the man behind us is Jim Richards. Are you related to Howard Hulland?"

"The son of a bitch is my brother, yes." The statement took us by surprise.

Lynn stepped forward and asked, "Have you seen your brother recently?"

"The bastard called me early this morning asking if he could stay with me for a day or two, I told him to go to hell."

"Did he say where he was staying?"

"Nope, I didn't ask either. He used to beat on our mother after our father died, I think he killed him but it couldn't be proven. I never forgave him for that treatment of our mom."

Lynn took out her card, gave it to the woman and asked, "If you see or hear from him, call me. See if you can find out where he is."

"If he's anywhere he's probably going to end up back at his ex-wife's home. He'll probably beat her into letting him stay. If you catch him, put some lead between his eyes." She gave us the location of the ex-wife and closed the door.

"I guess we're finished with her," Deacon said.

**

Chapter 21

Trapper took Sam's phone and tried the call back number, but it didn't work. He took out his cell phone and called his friend Josh at LVMPD, he answered after a couple rings.

"Now what do you want?" he said as Trapper laughed thinking about how he used to say the same thing to Jim when he would call for a favor.

"Can you get a trace on a cell phone for me? It's a missing person who just called asking for help. The call was short, about three seconds."

"Can you bring the phone in?"

"Yeah, we aren't far from you. I'll be there in a couple minutes. We'll probably also file a missing person's report, he's been gone for over five days. See you shortly." Trapper hung up and started the Jeep, then drove to Metro.

He took Sam in through the desk Sergeant who was happy to see Trapper. "What are you doing back here? Weber know you're in the house?"

"No and I plan on keeping it that way."

"Well if it's any consolation, Weber is busy with some big deal going on. I heard its terrorists, know anything about it?"

"Yeah, my associate Jim Richards is trying to stop a terrorist threatening to blow up Vegas," he said with a straight face.

"Really, I heard that. You here to see your buddy Josh Harper?"

"Yep, and I know the way, thanks Gil."

Trapper took Sam back to the squad room for missing persons and they found Josh standing by the coffee machine.

"I figured you'd come here first so I'm stealing their coffee. Want some of this swill?"

"No, I value my health. Josh this is my girlfriend Samantha Hathaway, Sam this is Josh Harper."

"You look familiar? Do I know you?"

"Only if you busted her," Trapper said with a laugh. "Never mind it's a long story. I'm going to leave Sam here to file a report, you and I can go see about the cell phone."

Josh asked a detective to take her report and call him when she was finished. The detective said he would and asked Sam to take a seat.

Trapper and Josh went through the building to the crime lab and into the electronics department. Josh went to a man sitting at a slew of computers and said, "Yoshi, this man is the immortal Will Trapper, formerly of the LVMPD and a thorn in Weber's side."

The Asian looking man smiled and said, "Yes, I know of Trapper's exploits last year pulling pranks on Weber around Vegas. Pleased to meet you. You are a legend in the precinct, I heard about the hookers in the holding cells, that was you?"

"Guilty, but I won't admit to it, to protect myself from incrimination."

Josh laughed, "Everyone knows it was you so you have been incriminated long ago. That's why Weber is always warning us to keep an eye on you since you moved back to Vegas."

"Glad I'm so infamous," Trapper said.

"Yoshi I need a fix on a location from a three second cell phone call, think you can do your magic and find the source?" Josh asked the tech.

"Where's the phone and I'll tell you?"

Trapper took the phone from his pocket and handed it to the tech. Yoshi studied the phone, taking the back off and pulling the SIM card. He slid it into some device on his console and typed a few things into the keyboard. The computer monitor came to life with graphs and symbols totally alien to Trapper. Yoshi poked and probed the computer for a bit, then the screen changed to show a triangle over a map of Las Vegas.

"This is the triangulation of the towers that sent the call. I'll try to narrow it down by signal strength to an exact location." He did some more typing until the screen showed a white box pointing to an area down in south Vegas, in the industrial section of town. Yoshi wrote down the address and handed it to Josh.

"You are a magician Yoshi," Trapper said as the tech was reassembling the phone.

"That's high praise from the prank master, I'll accept it." He smiled as Josh thanked him and took Trapper back to missing persons.

On the way Josh asked Trapper why his girlfriend looks so familiar to him. Trapper laughed and said, "She's an ex-hooker and now runs a bookie joint. Sound familiar now?"

"Oh hell yeah, I remember her now, back when she first started running numbers for Big Mike Carlino. She's a hot number herself, you should be proud."

"Oh, believe me, I am." They returned to missing persons and Sam was just finishing. "We may have a location on the call, let's go," Trapper said.

Josh asked, "Want me to tag along? I got nothing to do at the moment until they get a fix on this terrorist that has the precinct buzzing."

"Sure, you can pretend to be a cop and even use your gun if needed," Trapper laughed and they went out.

~~*~~

Lynn drove to the street where the house that Hulland's sister told us about. I could see there was a beat-up Chevy Nova in the drive and all the front curtains were drawn. Lynn sat in her car, I waited, then I saw her lift her cell phone and talk to someone. I waited to see what they were going to do. Deacon got out of the car and came back to me, I rolled down my window and he leaned in.

"Lynn called for back-up and a warrant, just in case he isn't here. No sense pissing off the ex-wife if he's not around. Just to make it legal. It shouldn't take too long to get a warrant since this is an Amber alert status for terrorist threat. They pull out the stops for bomb threats."

"Only Amber, I would have thought they would have it at red."

"They don't want to panic the public yet. Can you imagine trying to evacuate all the people in this town, the gamblers would never leave and the town would be grid locked worse than it already is."

Deacon stood as a couple of patrol cars came driving up behind us. I saw Detective Williams get out of the passenger side of one car. He came up and said to me, "Are you the person who stirred up all this mess?"

"I just got back from Area 51, brought a little excitement to this lackluster place," I said.

We waited until the warrant arrived, by then we had three more LVMPD black and whites and one SWAT van lining the street. I could see people peeking out of their windows wondering what was going down.

I told Lynn to warn everyone that there may be a boy in the building, so to proceed with caution. She passed along the info and organized the attack. She and Deacon went to the front door followed by a couple uniforms with SWAT holding back for word.

Lynn banged on the door, yelling police and that she had a search warrant, there was no response, so Lynn signaled the officer with the door ram to knock it in. He bashed the door and everyone poured in. I was by the front door, just outside and could hear the clear call being made.

Then I heard a loud yell for an EMS. I carefully went in and then as I went into the kitchen I saw a woman and a man lying on the floor. Lynn saw me and asked if I knew the man. I went close as she turned him, it was Fred Parnell, he was dead from a bullet to the back of the head. "He's the inside man I told you about, Fred Parnell. I guess Howie didn't need him anymore or he wanted a bigger share of the pie. Hulland is not a just evil, he's extremely evil. Especially any man who would bomb the hell out of a town of millions."

"I'm assuming the woman is Hulland's ex, she's still alive, barely. She's too out of it to talk." Lynn said. "I'll have a couple detectives go in with her to wait until she comes around. She may have some info."

The EMS techs came flying in and started to work on the woman. They brought in the gurney and put her on it and took her out to the ambulance. Two of Lynn's Detectives went into the vehicle for the ride in.

I walked around the house to see if I could find any sign of the boy, nothing popped.

Lynn found me and said, "A couple uniforms checked with neighbors and one woman across the street said she saw two men and a boy enter the house early this morning. They were in for a couple hours then one man left with the boy. We know the boy is still alive. We got the description of his vehicle and I put APB out on it. That's all we can do for now."

Deacon came to us with a piece of paper, "One of the guys found this taped to the fridge." He handed it to Lynn and she read it then handed it to me.

I read it aloud, "I'm sure you cops will track me this far, when you do tell that fucking P.I. Richards that I want the extra part, he knows what I want. I'll call him at his office at five P.M. today and he better be agreeable or the boy dies slowly and painfully."

I wasn't happy.

**

Chapter 22

Trapper followed Josh down the Vegas strip out past the Luxor and over to Industrial Drive south to where there stood industrial complexes. They arrived at a building that looked like a storefront but it had a sign saying it was the offices of the Bayward Clinic.

They departed their cars and went into the lobby of the building finding an empty desk. Trapper went to a door off the side and opened it finding a hallway leading to a couple more doors. Josh and Sam followed Trapper down the hall, when they heard a loud screaming sound. Both Trapper and Josh had their weapons out and Trapper told Sam to stay back.

They went to the door that the sounds came from and Trapper carefully opened it. They went in finding it to be an anteroom with another door. The screams were louder now and Trapper rushed the door and went in with his gun out front. Josh came up on his right and they saw a man strapped down to a table under surgical lights. There was a man with his back to them bending over a table of what looked like surgical tools.

"Hey!" Trapper yelled and surprised the man. He turned holding a large scalpel and saw the intruders, he had a mask on but it was easy to see he was surprised.

Josh held his badge up and said loudly, "Police, back off and get your hands up."

Trapper heard Sam behind him cry out, "Phillip, are you all right?"

The man on the table turned his head and saw Sam, but he looked drugged. The man in the surgical gown went to Phillip and held the scalpel to his neck. "Stay back or I'll cut his artery."

Josh quietly said, "Fuck you," and fired. The man's head jerked back from the bullet hitting him in the temple and he fell to the floor. They rushed to Phillip and started to undo the straps. Josh had his cell phone out and called for an EMS unit. Sam was hugging her brother and crying. He was safe now.

~~*~~

Area 51 Murders

We stood on the front lawn watching the neighbors standing on their porches or lawns watching the circus of cops, forensics techs, medical examiners, EMT's and detectives swarming in and around the house. I joked about charging admission, Lynn gave me her look. The one that says it isn't funny. She would give it to Deacon a lot, I got it a lot too. She had no sense of humor when it came to crime.

Joe Lang, Clark County medical examiner came up to us and handed me a piece of paper. "My bill for the jaunt out to alien country to do your autopsy. It was worth every penny."

I read the paper and smiled, "You are a capitalist above all. I'll pay this under protest, I'll send you a check. If I didn't need you so much I would have let your friend the funeral director do it."

"He's not qualified. Besides he can't make out a nice neat report like I can."

"I don't see any reference to hookers on this; did you have a boring night?"

"Do you really think Ash Springs has quality hookers, none I would want to indulge in. Also I want cash; your check is no good. Bring it to the morgue." Joe laughed and walked away.

"You borrowed the ME to go to Area 51 and do an autopsy?" Lynn asked.

"Yep, but I paid, so Clark County can relax. Are we good to go here, I should go to my office to wait for Hulland's call."

"Go ahead, we'll follow up shortly. You got an hour and a half before he calls. See you then."

I went to my car, drove back to my office, and parked in the back after waving to our guard at the back gate. I went in the building and checked Trapper's office, he wasn't there, I presumed he was still out looking for Sam's brother. I came to Buck's office; it was empty also. I felt alone.

I went to the lobby where I found Lacey, Penny and Willy all lounging in front of the television in the waiting area watching a recording of Penny's show.

"This is nice, if a client came in it would look like we have nothing better to do," I said with a grin.

Penny jumped up and latched on me with a big kiss, Willy was nipping at my ankle until I picked him up. We went back to the couches and sat. I noticed they had rearranged the furniture so it looked cozy like a living room rather than a business office lobby.

"I presume you are trying to make the clients feel at home and watching TV now."

Lacey spoke, "I read in Business Weekly that offices with a more homey arrangement makes for better client relations. So Penny and I did a little Feng Shui on the waiting area to make the clients relax. I'm relaxed, aren't you Penny?"

"Oh, I am so relaxed I could kick off my shoes and take a nap," she said with a big smile.

"Feng Shui? That's a fancy word for I'll charge you a fortune to set up your environment to be totally useless."

"Doesn't it make you feel more comfortable?" Lacey asked.

"Yes, I'm starting to feel it. Now if we can get back to work." I gave Lacey a look, she caught my hint, and she went back to her desk.

"Meanie," Penny said.

"I'm not paying for sitting around watching TV. How's Jessie doing?" I asked about the young girl left orphaned by the Vigilante killer, who we took in for a while before letting Lacey and Mac take her in after they married last month.

"She's doing well according to Lacey. Grades are good and finding new friends to associate with. I'm happy for her."

"I'm glad she found a good home with Lacey and Mac," I said as my cell phone rang. I excused myself and went to my office to answer, the caller ID said it was the sheriff from Lincoln County.

"Sheriff, how are you?" I asked.

"I'm good Jim, I just wanted to call and fill you in on Darryl," he said.

I felt a chill for some reason and asked, "Did you find him?"

"Yep, just off the side of Highway 375, at the end of the private road going to the base in Area 51. He was burned over most of his body. Can I bring him down to Vegas to be examined by your friend, the ME?"

"I'll call him but I'm sure it's possible. Make a formal request to the Vegas ME's office and I'm sure he'll do it. Besides I haven't paid him yet for coming out to Ash Springs, so I'll hold the payment till he helps you."

He laughed and continued, "Works for me. I have to get some ice for the back of our pickup truck to pack him in. He's toasty but I'll keep him fresh."

"I'll call and it will be good to see you in Vegas. Do you have a place to stay in town?"

"I'll just find a motel until I get a report to take back with the body for burial. The county will pay for the hole."

"Never mind a motel, I have a guest house you will stay at while you are here, besides I may need you to help find our psycho terrorist. I want you close by."

"I'll do what I can. I'll call when I'm getting into town," he said as he finished.

I dialed Joe Lang and he came on, "Are you coming to pay?" he asked.

"Are you in a rush for my money?"

Area 51 Murders

"Sure, you don't need it. Your wife is rich, you can retire and live comfortably," he laughed.

"Don't let her hear that. I need another job from you, this time official. The Lincoln County Sheriff is bringing a body to be autopsied. The man was burned badly and found out by area 51. He's a Native American."

"Let me know when he's coming in, I'll take care of it personally."

"You're comfortable with it?"

"I'm Native American, on my mother's side. I give priority to the tribes in the area, just let me know."

"Thanks Joe, will do." We finished and hung up.

I sat at my desk and wondered how I could get into such fantastic adventures. Aliens, murder, kidnapping, total destruction of a city that never sleeps. And why? I knew that Penny had this theory of how death and murder follows me, I would humor her, but I really wondered if she was right.

My cell phone rang again and it said private. I answered; it was the Captain from Nellis who the Major said would be in contact. "What can I do for you Captain?"

"Well, you are the man who Hulland wants, you tell me what I can do for you."

"Are you in the area?"

"Yes, I'm outside your office. I didn't want to come in to blow any operation you may have going," he said.

I laughed to myself thinking how careful the military can be. All operations and setups. "I have a lot to tell you, come in and we'll talk." I went out and told Penny that the military was here to visit so I would be busy.

She said she was going to watch the TV with Willy and Lacey. I just rolled my eyes and went back to my office.

The back door opened and the Captain came in with two other persons I assumed were SID agents. I was surprised that they came in through the back door, they knew more about my office than I figured. I invited them to come into my private office and asked them to sit.

**

Chapter 23

The rather military looking man identified himself as Captain Goodson, the name the Major gave me. He had on Air Force dress blues and a chest full of brass and ribbons. As a commander in SID I figured he would arrive here undercover, but he evidently liked to play soldier. He sent his men to the front of the building and remained standing at parade rest in my office. I sat at my desk, waiting for him to sit, he didn't.

He asked for a report, I stifled a chuckle, and I started to explain what we had been doing locally to find Hulland, he stood nodding as I talked.

"So you have to be in contact with Hulland by five, correct?"

"Yes, that's his demands, I'm just waiting."

"Why does he want to talk to you? He could just go on with his quest to set up his plot to set off the bomb he has and that would be that?"

"Well, it's not that simple, I kept out one of the three parts he needs to set off the bomb to destroy Vegas. He knows it now and wants to tell me his demands for the safe return of Mitchell Huston for the final piece of the bomb."

"Well, we'll need that part you have."

"Nope, I have to use it to negotiate the safe return for Mitchell."

"It's not negotiable. That vial is property of the United States government. You have to return it to me or face treason charges yourself."

"You have no sense of humor or sense of justice do you?" I stood and went around to him. "Do you enjoy seeing a nine year old child being tortured or murdered for a demand?"

"It's not just a single child, it's millions of people dying at the hands of an fanatic. Even Spock said the needs of the few out way the needs of the many."

I was amazed he used the Spock reference. "You are evil aren't you?" I said.

He laughed and said, "I'm not evil, just trying to be reasonable. Following the letter of the law."

"The letter of the law has been proven to be wrong many times, hasn't it?"

"Well, it has been proven to be wrong many times, yes, but you have a dangerous part of a biological weapon that will wipe out many people if let loose."

"I have it hidden very well, and I won't let it loose without a good reason. You can depend on it. Hulland wants to complete his threat of destroying Las Vegas, I won't let him. I don't want the boy to be hurt, but I do think about the bigger picture. I'll have to be trusted to work this out, or give a crazed terrorist the part to murder millions. Putting me up next to Him. I don't think so. Besides if I give him the vial, he won't be able to use it.

"What does that mean?

I filled him in on my plan, and he was pacified for now.

~~*~~

Area 51 Murders

The EMT's had Phillip on the gurney, he was okay except for the drugs the doctor had given him. Trapper, Sam and Josh were standing by as Sam asked him a question.

"Phil, what is going on?"

"I'm sorry Sam, for not confiding in you. I never told you about my gender preference and I asked for the money to pay back the loan shark I borrowed from to have the sexual reassignment surgery. The original operation was canceled and then I couldn't pay back the loan shark so I asked you for the money. You turned me down. I finally found this clinic that would do the operation but didn't realize until he had me captive that it's an organ mill. He was going to harvest my organs to sell on the black market. Plus he took the money I borrowed. I was brought to this room for him to start cutting, but he had to go out for something and he thought I was knocked out from his drugs, I was still awake but barely. He had left his cell phone on the desk in the room so I called you but he came back before I could tell you where I was. He was mad and strapped me to the table. He said he was going to cut me apart while I was still awake for what I had done. I'm sorry Sam."

Sam comforted her brother and then the EMT's needed to take him in to be checked. Sam said she was going along with her brother. Trapper asked the EMT's where they were taking him and then said he'd see her later. They left leaving Josh and Trapper to explain the situation to the officers and CSI who arrived to secure the scene.

Josh turned to Trapper, "All in a day's work."

"Yep, and you are pretty handy with a gun," Trapper said as they searched the office.

Trapper found the files in the doctor's office containing a good number of details pertaining to his recent surgeries and his sales to various people around the states. "The doctor either was stupid to keep all the facts so handy or he was saving them in case his operation was compromised," Trapper said.

Josh examined a number of boxes in a rather large freezer that held body parts from who knows who?

"Judging from the number of boxes I'd say the doc was busy hiding lots of bodies. I'm sure the desert is full of recently dug holes. We'll never know now will we?"

"Well, you shot him in the head, it's a good bet he's not going to tell us now," Trapper said with a laugh.

"I saw a deadly threat against a human and took action. I will have to spend a lot of time before IA and a counselor explaining my actions but it was worth it. One less scum bag in the world." Josh grinned and winked at Trapper.

"You know you scare me sometimes."

"Yeah, sometimes I scare myself. Maybe I'll retire from the force and become a P.I. like you. I hear they get all the good looking women."

"Just keep your mitts off Sam, she's my good looking woman. I'm handy with a gun also and you know it."

~~*~~

Lynn and Deacon arrived around four-thirty and I introduced them to the Captain. His men were in the lobby sitting with Penny and Lacey watching the TV. I tried not to laugh at the sight of the men in black watching Penny's talk show, but they seemed enthralled with watching Penny trying to do a balancing act with members of the Circus-Circus Casino entertainers.

"So what's the plan of attack?" Lynn asked.

"I just wait and see, Hulland has most of the cards, but I have the aces. Hopefully he will be willing to exchange the boy for what I have."

"You're going to give him the one thing he needs to wipe out Las Vegas, for the boy?" Deacon said.

"I have every confidence that he's not going to destroy anything. I just want the boy back to his mother. So don't fret about dying anytime soon."

"Jim, you worry me sometimes. I've let you have your way in past situations and you come out smelling rosy, but I worry about this. From what I've found out about this guy, he's nuts and a loose cannon," Lynn said with a worried look on her face. "I've got family here and I don't want them dead."

"As I said, don't worry." I heard the phone up front ring and then Lacey called back to say it was for me. I told everyone to be quiet; I was putting it on the speakerphone. I answered.

"Hello?"

"Richards, you thought you were cute back in Rachel when you tripped up Dylan. He's not going to be talking anymore, I've dealt with him like I did with Fred. Fred filled me in on everything you were up to. I'm ready to deal with you too, or I'll cut the boy to pieces and send them back to his mother."

"Come on Howie, you do that and you lose. You have the formula; you don't need to mass murder people to prove your point. What are you trying to do, move up the ladder from Hitler. You know you will be hunted forever by the entire forces of the United States. You won't be able to enjoy your money from the sale of the formula if you have to be hiding all the time."

"I got plans for what I'll do after I pull off the biggest incident in history. Bigger than the bombs at Hiroshima and Nagasaki. Gee, did we try anyone for the mass murder of all those millions of people? Huh? I'm going to be welcome in any enemy country of the U.S. where they won't be able to touch me. I can live anywhere comfortably. The destruction of Vegas is my personal vendetta and I won't weep over the bodies of it's people. Now let's stop wasting time and get down to the gory details of this trade. I really don't care about the boy but you do. So I'll be willing to trade. Now take me off your speakerphone, I don't need the military people and your cop friends to hear what I have to say to you. Do it now!"

I was surprised that he knew, he must be outside somewhere watching my office to have seen these people come in. I could see the expressions on everyone's faces as they realized the same thing.

I gave them a resigned look and took the phone off speaker. "Okay smart ass, what now?" I said into the phone.

I listened for a bit then hung up. "What did he say?" asked the Captain.

"He told me to keep my mouth shut and leave the office by myself. If he sees anyone follow, he'll cut a couple fingers off the boy's hand. Sorry guys but I have to do this myself."

**

Chapter 24

I drove out following the directions Hulland gave me. I had the vial in a zip lock bag on the seat next to me and I wasn't going to give it to him without the boy. I drove around to the back of the Mandalay Bay Hotel and pulled into the parking structure. I went up to the third level parking and over to the Vegas strip side of the building. I parked and got out of my car putting the vial in my coat pocket. I stood waiting when I saw a panel door open on the side of a van, Hulland got out.

"You got what I want?" he yelled to me.

I pulled the baggie out and waved it to him. He reached in the van and pulled the boy out. His hands were tied behind him and he had duct tape over his mouth. He looked panicked and thin, I was mad that Hulland must have treated him poorly. Hulland had a gun to his head.

"Now what?" I asked.

"You're the big shot P.I. you tell me how you want it to go down. You have more to lose than I do."

I looked the situation over, I was standing by the opening to the outside overlooking the strip, next to the waist high retaining wall that kept cars from dropping below. I said, "I'm going to put the vial on this wall, I'll go over there and you come get the thing. You can keep your gun on the boy and then you can go off that way behind the ramp down."

"Leaving my van here?"

"You'll be rich enough to buy a fleet."

"What's to say I won't kill the boy after I get the vial?"

I reached behind my back, pulled my Glock from my belt, and held it up pointing at him. "Because I will shoot you if you don't leave us peacefully. I only want the boy; I could give a shit for you."

163

"Fair enough, now move away from the vial." I walked to a row of cars to his right and he moved around leaving the boy standing by the van but keeping his eye and gun on the boy. I had my Glock up and pointed at him. I could have taken a shot but the distance I was at, I might have missed, then he could kill the boy. He went up quickly and grabbed the vial then he studied it. He looked back to me and smiled, I was worried he would screw up my plan. He didn't. Then he did something that surprised me, he jumped over the retaining wall and disappeared over the side of the building.

I ran to the boy and cut his bonds with my pocket knife after removing the tape on his mouth. He remembered me from when we met at his mother's. I took him to my car and told him to get on the floor in the back until I said otherwise, he did. I ran over to the retaining wall and looked down, I didn't see Hulland, but I saw a large truck with a bunch of mattresses in the back. He knew this would happen, if I said otherwise, he would have led me back to the wall so he could complete his plan. I guess I didn't give him enough credit.

I pulled out my cell phone, called Lynn and told her I had the boy. I left quickly before he could come back.

I had Mitch safely in my office and put him on the phone to his mother. I could tell she was tearfully happy as was the boy. I went out to the lobby and saw a pickup truck pull up to the building, it was the sheriff. He got out and came in. I didn't say anything just motioned for him to follow me. I took him to my office door and he saw Mitch.

"Well done Jim. I presume he's talking to Louise?"

"Yep, do you have Darryl in your truck?"

"Oh hell no, I already took him by the morgue, they have a real nice setup there. Good to have funds to afford it. Joe Lang was more than nice to help get Darryl into his place. Joe said Darryl had what looked like radiation burns but he'd have more conclusive results later. Is Hulland in custody?"

"No, he's still out there, but we got Mitch back, that was my goal, now the military and the police can go after Hulland."

"I'm sure he'll be found, but doesn't he have the vial to pull off his plan, should I get the hell out of town?" he said with a smile.

"No, Hulland thinks he has the virus in the vial but he doesn't. He's going to be pissed when his bomb fizzles. I'll explain it later. Now I have to see about getting Mitch back to his mother."

I took the sheriff to the lobby again where everyone was congregated. I did introductions all around and asked Lynn, "Do you have anyone willing to drive out to Rachel to take Mitch back home?"

"I'm sure I can find a black and white sitting outside of a donut shop. Leave it to me." She went off to make a call as I kissed Penny and let Willy doggy kiss me. I was happy for now, but Hulland still had to be caught.

Area 51 Murders

~~*~~

Sam was sitting by Phillip's bedside in the hospital, as Trapper walked in. Sam introduced Trapper, as he pulled a chair over and sat. Trapper took out an envelope from his jacket and handed it to Phillip.

"What's this?" he asked.

"Well, don't make a big deal out of it; I sort of stole it from evidence at the clinic. It's your money that the doc took from you and you need to get back to Rancid Ricky. I'll take you over to convince him that you are paid in full, when you're ready."

"Thank you so much, I can't express my appreciation enough for what Sam told me you did."

"Actually I didn't do that much without the help of the Metro PD and my friend Josh Harper. But I'm glad we found you in time or you would have been spread all over the place."

"Yeah I did a stupid thing."

"No, you were misguided and conned by a very bad person. He murdered many people to steal their body parts and we found a list of dig sites he used, they will be finding the bodies and hopefully closing a few missing person's reports. It was good you managed to get to the phone."

Bob Moats

Sam leaned to her brother and said, "Phil, do you really want the surgery to complete you as a woman?"

Phil teared up and said, "It's something I've wanted for years, I hate being in this shell, I need to free me."

Sam was quiet for a short time; Trapper took her hand and squeezed it. She looked to him and then back to her brother. "Phil, Will's going to help you take back the money you borrowed and then we will get you in a reputable clinic to have your surgery. I'm taking care of it; I've always wanted a sister."

~~*~~

Everyone had left the office, except the sheriff, it was quiet now. The military was going off to see if they could track Hulland. Lynn and Deacon went out to do the same and Lynn had a patrol car take Mitch back to his mom. I was happy and sitting on the couch with Penny as Lacey was typing something at her desk. The sheriff was sitting in a chair next to the couch and said, "You private eyes have it easy."

"I wouldn't trade this job for anything else, but it's not all that easy."

"So how did you do the switch on Hulland with the vial?"

"Well I stopped at a drugstore for a specimen bottle and then at home I put the bottle, the vial and a small travel size bottle of talcum powder in a big zip lock bag. I sealed the bag well and then through the plastic I opened the vial, poured the contents into the specimen bottle and closed it. Then I poured the talc into the vial and sealed it back. I put the vial into another zip bag and sealed it. I took the vial out of the big bag and sealed it back up. I put the real virus in my garage and took the fake one to give to Hulland. At the parking structure he looked at the vial but only saw powder that he thought was the virus. I hoped he didn't know that the real virus was a bit orangish and the talc was white, but he bought the whole thing and went off, leaving Mitch."

"Brilliantly done, my hat's off to you."

"Yeah but he may not like being fooled. Can you put a man on Louise and the boy until Hulland is caught?"

"You think he'd go all the way back there to get revenge?"

"I don't know what he may do, but let's not take chances. Well, shall we get you settled into our guest house?"

"Sounds good to me, I hate motels, so this will be nice."

Penny went to get her purse from my office and I told Lacey to pack it in for the night. She agreed and was out of the door before Penny even finished getting ready to go. "I guess she wanted to go see Mac." I told Penny when she came out. Penny went to her car and I went to mine.

Bob Moats

We drove out to the house with the sheriff following. We pulled into the drive and I put the car into the garage, Penny parked her car in next to mine. The sheriff parked in the drive and we all went into the house. Penny let Willy loose and said she was going to the pool after she changed.

"Mighty pretty wife you got there Jim."

"Yeah, I think I'll keep her."

"Where is this guest house you told me about I'd like to freshen up."

"Sure, come with me." I led him out the back door to the house off the side of our home and took him in. "It's not big, but it's comfy."

"It's fine with me, I'm just going to rest for a while, does that TV work?"

"Sure we have satellite TV so just turn it on and enjoy, but stay away from the porn." I laughed and left him to do his thing.

**

Chapter 25

Later, around eight o'clock, we invited the sheriff into our living room to relax and talk. I asked the sheriff if he would like a beer.

"Does cactus grow in the desert?" he laughed.

"I'll take that as a yes," I said and handed him a can. I gave Penny her can and I sat. Willy was sitting on the floor just staring at the sheriff, I was wondering what Willy was thinking.

"So have you heard from Joe Lang about Darryl?"

"Yes, he called me a little while ago and said that Darryl was exposed to high concentrations of radiation. His body gave a little registration on the Geiger counters but not enough to cause problems for people who came in contact with the body. I made sure all my men who handled Darryl were wearing gloves."

"I wonder how he got the exposure?"

"Joe asked if we really had aliens out our way. I said I doubted that Darryl was abducted by little green men. The base has areas where they store radioactive materials, Darryl may have stumbled on one of the restricted areas."

"But why was his body dumped in the desert and why so it could be found?"

"That's a mystery we'll probably never know, unless the people who did it fess up to it. My theory is Darryl escaped again and walked to the area we found him, keeled over from the radiation and died. Oh and Louise called me, she was so delirious about Mitch's safe return she asked me to thank you."

"I'm glad I could help, I hope Hulland is found so we can all rest." The television was on in the background but we weren't watching it, the sound was turned down low. I would glance over every now and then and suddenly saw a face I knew, it was Hulland. I grabbed the remote and hiked up the volume.

The news person was talking about the image of Hulland saying, "If any person sees this man, do not go near him, report his whereabouts to the police. This man is armed and dangerous, he has murdered two people already. Police and the military are hunting him and would appreciate the public to be on the lookout also. At the top of the sports news..." I turned the sound off.

"Well the manhunt continues," I said. I was wondering if Hulland knew where I lived. I would have to sleep with my Glock nearby.

"Hulland won't know if the vial I gave him was fake until he tries to use it. After that failure, he won't look good in the eyes of the terrorist who are bidding on the product." I said.

My cell phone rang and I saw it was Lynn. I excused myself from the room and went to the kitchen. "Hello Lynn," I said as I answered.

Area 51 Murders

"Jim, We're working with your Captain Goodson and his people say that Hulland has been posting his threats on the internet to a group of militant factions and is now trying to take bids for the formula for the bomb. We were trying to get a fix on the IP address but it may not do much good. They say he looks to be working from a laptop with a wireless broadband modem, so he could be anywhere. I just wanted to let you know what was going on. You haven't heard from him have you?"

"If I had, you'd be the first to know. Wireless broadband works just like a cell phone, can't they get a fix on his location by triangulating the tower signals?"

"We tried that but he's moving around too much. I'd say he has another van and is using it to hide his whereabouts. This man is clever."

"Dangerous also. Keep me informed, I'm in need of a good night's sleep in my own bed. The beds out in Area 51 were a little hard for my liking. I'll call you in the morning unless you come up with something. Call me."

She agreed and we hung up. I looked out to the living room to Penny and the sheriff talking, and had an odd feeling, that Hulland may be near. Now I wouldn't be able to sleep well. Damn Hulland.

I went out and told Penny and the sheriff what Lynn had said and I would check the internet later to see what this was all about. I was wearing down and said so.

We said our good nights to the sheriff and he went off to the guesthouse. I warned him about the alarm sensors around the property so if he hears horns going off then to be prepared for the worse. He said he'd sleep with his gun and then went off.

Penny and I climbed into bed and she cuddled me. I was whipped and said to Penny, "I haven't had sex with you in almost a week, but can we hold off one more night? Between my lack of sleep up in Rachel and worrying about Hulland being loose, I'm really not in a sexy mood."

She smiled and kissed my cheek saying, "Get a good night sleep and I'll attack you later. I'll just roll over and think of Eric."

"I'm so tired I won't even comment on Eric. But I better not hear you moaning." I felt the bed shake from her stifled laughter and turned on my side.

I laid there for what seemed like an eternity, then I felt hungry. Fine time for food, it was now three-thirty. I quietly got up and went to the kitchen and raided the fridge. I was assembling a ham sandwich when I heard a noise in the garage area. I went to the door to the garage and opened it slowly, listening for any more noises. I heard a quiet rustling in my workshop area and turned on the lights. I was shocked to see the sheriff stand up looking to me. He pulled his gun and told me to step into the garage. I stupidly left my Glock in the bedroom when I went to get my food. I went into the garage and he came around the cars and stopped by the mini-limo I owned.

"I had hoped to do this without you finding out, but now I don't have to dig around for the virus, you can take me to it."

"Son of a bitch. I trusted you, how long have you been working with Hulland?" I asked.

"I'm not working with him, and I haven't. But since you have the extra ingredient for the bomb I figured I'd make a little profit too. Sorry Jim, I liked you, but I got to do what I can to make myself a little richer. I was hoping to find the stuff and get out of your way, but this puts a crimp on that. Now you know, so I have to decide what to do. Before I decide your fate, please show me the virus."

"And if I refuse?"

"Then that pretty wife of yours won't be so pretty when I get done with her. Just give me what I want and I'll be on my way. Please don't make me shoot either of you."

I thought about the options, I didn't want to give him the material but I didn't want Penny or myself to die. My mind flashed back to the Captain's reference to Spock. My few were important to me, but the needs of the many were important too. I wasn't going to give it to him.

He was watching me, and said, "I've studied people all my life and I'm a good reader of expressions. You know where the virus is, right?"

I did a stupid thing, I glanced at the locker under my workbench. He smiled and said, "I was right, thanks for telling me." He went to the locker and opened it digging through the items in it, watching me and then he found the zip lock bag with the specimen jar of virus and the talc bottle.

He held it up and said, "I don't want to hurt you. So if you could sit on that chair next to your workbench, I'd appreciate it. Please remember your lovely wife and don't do anything stupid."

I sat as he came around behind me and I heard him ripping out a length of duct tape and wrapped it around my wrists. Then he put a short piece across my mouth and then ran the roll around my waist and chair.

He came around the front of me and said, "I'll just be taking my leave. You'll probably be found by your wife in the morning when she comes out to go to work. I'll be long gone by then, thanks Jim, it's been fun." I heard him go to the door at the side of the garage that leads out to the guesthouse. About five minutes later I heard the door to the guesthouse slam and then he went around the front of the house, but he forgot about the alarms. The light sensors flooded the front yard and the alarms were going off loud enough to wake the dead. He must have ran to his truck as I heard him drive out.

A few minutes later, Penny came rushing out with her Smith and Wesson .38 that we bought her during the Sin City murder case, and she came into the garage when she saw the open door. She ran her gun back and forth to see if I was alone then came to me and pulled the tape from my mouth.

"What the hell happened?" she asked as she cut my bonds with hedge clippers from the wall.

"The sheriff is a bad guy, I have to call Lynn, he's got the virus."

Chapter 26

"Yeah, Lincoln County Sheriff Billy Davis has the bottle with the virus, he blindsided me and took it. Says he's not working for Hulland, he's freelancing the virus to get rich, but I have an idea that he's going to end up dead."

I was talking to Captain Goodson who was at LVMPD where they set up a military command center to catch Hulland. "Damn, I wish you had given us the virus yesterday instead of bringing it in today. This would never have happened. This is not good. How is Davis going to contact Hulland to offer him the thing?"

"I think he may try going online since he knows that Hulland has set up a website. Try watching that for any attempts. I'll be at the station shortly." I hung up feeling worse that they had the real virus. I hoped the sheriff would screw up and get caught before he did something stupid.

Penny called in sick for her show, she wanted to be with me today, just in case. I didn't object. I called Lacey and told her that she and Mac should take Jessie and go far out of town in case Hulland gets the third ingredient. I couldn't say when he might try to use the bomb, but it's better to be safe. Lacey said she had a cousin in Flagstaff, Arizona. I said that would be far enough and said to go soon. I called Buck and told him the story, he refused to leave town, he wanted to help catch Hulland. I admire Buck for his loyalties. I got dressed and Penny and I drove out to Metro. Penny had Willy in his purse, she wanted him nearby also.

We arrived at Metro and went in to Lynn's office. She wasn't there, Williams walked by and said they all were in the conference room where they set up the command center. We went to the room and stopped just outside as I saw the mayor of Las Vegas talking to Captain Goodson.

"How the hell does a biological weapon get into Vegas?" he was yelling.

"It's a terrorist plot, they are trying to use Vegas as an example to show the strength of this weapon," the Captain calmly replied. "The man behind this is taking bids online for the formula and so far there are responses from factions in Iran and Afghanistan. The Palestinians are chiming in also."

"Jesus H. Christ! Is this nut going to set the thing off and should we evacuate the city?"

The Captain stared at him and said, "Mr. Mayor, pardon me, but are you delusional? This town is gridlocked most the time; an evacuation would cause as many deaths as the bomb. We just have to put all our men on this to find the nut, as you call him. Please just let us do our job or get out of town. I'm in touch with the Pentagon on this and we may put Vegas under martial law."

The mayor looked flustered, just shook his head and stormed out. Penny and I went in and up to Lynn standing in a corner of the room, trying to hide I presumed. She smiled at me and asked, "Is he gone?"

"Yep, he flew by me and down the hall. Anything brewing?"

"We're watching the website Hulland set up and he's getting plenty of hits for the bidding."

Captain Goodson saw me and came over, "Well Richards, any good ideas now?" he snipped at me.

"If Sheriff Davis does manage to get the virus to Hulland, he would only be able to set it off for maximum effect by being up high in the air, higher the better I'm told. First you should ground all aircraft private or commercial and have jets flying or standing by to intercept any rouge planes."

The Captain blinked a few times and turned to his men and yelled, "Put a lock down on all aircraft, contact McCarran Airport and warn them to reroute all private aircraft or commercial planes, jets, kites, anything that flies to stay away from Vegas until further notice. They will be shot down. Call air command at Nellis and tell them to be ready to scramble fighter jets with incendiary missiles to vaporize the bastard and his cargo. Jump now!"

His men scrambled to get to the extra phones they had installed and were making their calls. He turned back to me, "Okay, now what?"

"Well, Hulland is getting everyone worked up with his website, once he gets a good amount of bids he'll do the deed. I'd shut down the web servers and pull his plug to squelch his thunder. No bidders, no call to beat his chest."

Captain Goodson turned to Captain Weber who showed up after the mayor left and said. "You need to get with my computer tech and find out what ISP Hulland is going through, then I'll have my contacts get you an executive order to shut down the webhost till we get Hulland. If they object tell them we will attack with tanks."

I was beginning to wonder if the Captain had any brains at all to figure all these simple plans. He looked to me again, I shrugged my shoulders and said, "That's all I got for now."

He turned on his heels and went to the other side of the room where his people were huddled. Weber gave me a smile and went to talk to the tech on the computers.

Lynn said, "Where do we begin to look? Hulland seems to be on the move, not staying in one spot very long."

A voice yelled from the computer center set up to watch Hulland's website, "Captain, I've got a message from the sheriff to Hulland. Lynn and I went to the table and I came up behind the tech reading over his shoulder.

The message read, "Hulland, I'm Lincoln County Sheriff Davis, you don't have the virus, Richards conned you by giving you a vial filled with talcum powder, I have the real virus and I want to negotiate its return to you, but for a reward. I want one million dollars and the third part is yours. You are going to look stupid if you try to set off the bomb now. Contact me at BillyDLC@lcsheriffs.com to arrange for the trade."

Area 51 Murders

"The sheriff is goading Hulland, he may be in for a rude awakening. We need to access that email address to see what they are going to do," Lynn said.

"Wait, there's a reply," the tech said.

I looked again to the computer and read, "Davis, if you are lying to me, I'll personally take pleasure in killing you. I'll contact you for a swap, but I need to get the money. I'll tell you when," was all the reply said.

"This is going to delay the attack for a while longer while they fight to figure out how to swap. But Hulland is clever, he proved that to me when I swapped the talc for Mitchell. If you can hack into the servers to read the email it would help," I said to the tech.

"Normally that's illegal to hack into a webserver, but," he looked to the Captain who nodded, "I suppose under the conditions, I can be forgiven."

He did what he could to find a way into the servers for the email. The host was in a small building just outside Las Vegas. I knew this because I looked into email servers for the firm.

The tech worked his fingers then he said he got the most recent emails. He printed them out and Captain Goodson took them, reading, "Sheriff, I will call you. Give me a number." Then he read from the next paper, "Call me at 555-4758 and we'll make arrangements." The Captain threw the papers down, "We won't be able to get the phone call traced in time, and they probably have already talked and made arrangements. Damn."

~~*~~

An hour later the sheriff stood at the top of the ramp in the parking structure waiting for Hulland to arrive or show himself if he was already hiding out watching from nearby. Earlier he had planted the virus bottle in a hiding place in the building, where he knew Hulland wouldn't find it without him telling the location. The sheriff was feeling a little sad that he had to resort to this but he was fed up with his meager life in the desert. This was a good chance for him to start over somewhere else and get his life together. He heard a click behind him and slowly turned to see Hulland pointing a gun at his head from across the aisle standing between two cars.

"Well, Sheriff, shall we do business?"

"You really think you can get away with this? Destroying millions of people, you'll be hunted forever you know. The government won't even worry about foreign protocol for tracking you down and killing you in cold blood where ever you stand."

"I have friends in Muslim extremist nations that will protect me, for providing them the solution to wipe out their enemies. I'm not worried."

"Enemies? Just who are the enemies? We're the enemy to many people, just as the followers of the Jihad is ours. Once they start wiping out nations who will be left to run the place? They'll all start to fight amongst themselves and they will become their own worst enemy."

"Stop talking political rhetoric to me, I don't need you to preach or try to convert me. Just give me the virus and we can be on our way. How shall we do this?"

"Well, I'm not here to cheat you, I just want my money so I can get out of town while you bring it to ruin. I do have the virus put in a safe place nearby and as soon as you fork over the cash, I'll tell you where it is."

Hulland stood motionlessly, then reached down next to the car and picked up a large gym bag. He placed it in front of him and said, "Now where is it?"

"Open the bag and pull out a handful so I can see it's real and not paper."

Hulland grinned, "You don't trust me old man?"

"Nope."

Hulland reached down, unzipped the bag, took out a couple stacks of cash, and waved it to the sheriff. "Good enough?"

"Yep, now you can go get your virus. It's sitting on top of that junction power box on the wall over there." He pointed to the box and smiled, "Now go get your prize, as I get mine."

Hulland started to walk towards the box as the sheriff was going to get the bag. He picked up the bag and turned to see Hulland aim and fire three shots into his chest from across the aisle; he dropped down next to a car and remained still. Hulland was satisfied, went to the box, and took the bag holding the powder from the top of the box. He looked back to the body of the sheriff still prone on the floor and laughed. Then he went out.

**

Chapter 27

About five minutes later, the sheriff carefully lifted his head and listened for any sound. Hearing none, he pulled himself up and stood looking around. He didn't see Hulland, then he pulled the three slugs from the bullet-proof vest he had under his uniform shirt and put them in his pocket, a souvenir of his day. He reached down and grabbed the cash bag that Hulland forgot in his haste, and then walked down the ramp to the ground level. He slowly and carefully walked to his pickup truck that he left on the ground floor parking. He drove out of the structure and turned down towards the Vegas Boulevard. He glanced down at the holes in his shirt from the bullets and chuckled. He looked to his badge he still had on and reached up to take it off. As he drove out of town on the length of desert highway south of the city, he tossed the badge out the window and didn't look back.

~~*~~

Area 51 Murders

Buck called me from outside the precinct; he still wasn't fond of cop shops. I told him to wait out there for me, and went to get Penny while she stood looking lost in the middle of the crowded room. We went out the back door, into the parking lot and found Buck leaning on his T-Bird.

"Buck my good friend; I need to ask you for a really big favor."

"Name it."

"I need you to take Maria and Penny and drive down to Bullhead City and find a motel for a couple of days until we catch Hulland."

Penny spoke up, "Hey, I'm not leaving you, just forget that. I'm sticking around to protect my investment. Besides, if you died, I don't really want to have to break in another old fart like you as a husband. I'm not going, so don't even think it. Buck you should think about taking Maria out of town though, you guys are still young and need to live."

"I've already talked to Maria about it, she says she wants to stay, if I'm staying and her brother is staying, she's staying."

"Yeah but Deacon is a cop and has to find Hulland, otherwise I'm sure he would take Maria out of town to be sure his sister is safe," I said.

"Yeah, well it's up to her and she says she's staying. Besides she has faith in us to catch the bad guy, we always do."

He gave us his big grin and I said, "Fine, but you have to come in the building. I'm not working this out with you in the parking lot."

"Deal," he said and we went in and back to the conference room.

After Buck and Penny were seated in the big conference room, I got out my cell phone and called Trapper. He came on and I asked where he was.

"I'm in the office, where is everyone?"

"I told Lacey to take Mac and Jessie out of the city and Buck is here with me. Hulland has the third part of the bomb so we are all trying to catch him before he lets it loose. Did you find your missing brother?"

"Yep and shut down a human organ donor mill. Has Hulland made his threat yet?"

"No, we are waiting to see what he does, we have no idea where he is but we're hoping some coincidence will occur and he'll be spotted. Maybe you should think about getting Sam out of town along with yourself."

"And let you have all the glory when you catch the psycho minutes before he detonates the bomb saving millions of people. Not on your life, I want to see that. Where are you at?"

"Metro, it's a little crazy here, there are military personnel spread out in the conference room taking calls about sightings of Hulland from the public and they have a

185

web watch going for his bidding, but they're going to pull the plug on that shortly. Hulland's got some heavy hitting bad guys from around the world all drooling to take control of the formula. This could be the end of life as we know it."

"Well, Sam is with her brother in the hospital, I'm not doing anything right now so I'll come by and give Weber something else to worry about."

I laughed and said, "See you shortly." I hung up and went to Penny and Buck. Lynn came over and said, "We're getting calls from all over Vegas in response to the TV news breaks looking for Hulland. They still haven't mentioned about the danger yet, no sense in panicking everyone. We got a couple good leads and there are men going there now."

My cell phone rang and caller ID said it was Trapper. "Forget something?"

"I was just leaving the building and the office phone rang, it was Hulland, he wants to talk to you. I wouldn't give him your number so he gave me his, convenient. Take this down."

I grabbed a note pad from a nearby desk and said to go ahead. I wrote the number and said I'd see him soon. I called Lynn back and told her what just happened.

"Before you call let's set up a trace on the number," she said.

"Go ahead, but if he was that willing to give it out, it must be a disposable phone, but you can try." Lynn talked to Captain Goodson and they got the computer geek to set up the trace. Goodson nodded to me and I placed the call.

It rang twice and I heard Hulland's voice, "Richards, I have to hand it to you for having the balls it took to switch the virus. I didn't do my homework good enough to know what I was looking at. Well played. But I have all the toys now to do my job."

"What happened to the sheriff?" I broke in to find out.

"That old fool won't be making any more deals. You can find his body on the third level parking at O'Sheas."

I was sorry to hear that, I actually like the sheriff; he was just blinded by greed.

Hulland continued, "I'm letting you know that you have twenty-four hours to stop me. But you won't, so make your arrangements for your demise and kiss your family good bye. I'm not talking long enough for you to trace this call, so take care and good-bye," he said, laughed and hung up.

I played back the recording my Palm Treo cell phone makes of all my calls and let everyone hear it.

"He's giving us twenty-four hours; he must be waiting for something to go down," I said, "Maybe he's going to contact his bidders to give them a time to watch for it. Just to prove he's behind it."

Area 51 Murders

Lynn said she'd send a car to O'Sheas parking to see about the sheriff. I was glad for that.

A young enlisted airman came up to the Captain and said something to him, Goodson said something back and the airman went to the door of the room and out. Goodson turned back to us and said, "Major Rickson has sent one of the biochemical scientists to fill us in on how this virus is going to go down."

The airman returned with a rather plump looking bald man with round spectacles and a bright red nose. I hoped from drinking and not from some virus. "Captain, I'm Rufus Segwill, Military Bio Division. I understand that a quantity of chemicals have been taken from Groom Lake base and are being use to threaten the city, am I correct?"

"Yes, you are correct; can you tell us what is involved to set this bomb off?"

"Well it's not really a bomb in that respect, it is just a meeting of three ingredients that cause a reaction that aids the spread of a virus. The three parts consist of two chemicals that when combined cause a reaction of particles that expand tremendously fast and over a wide area. These two chemicals bond with the virus molecules and carry the particles of the virus along with the expanding cloud of gas created. The gas can, from a great height, spread for many miles, depending of course on the weather conditions. Wind can have a factor as can rain. But under ideal conditions like there are in Las Vegas, the entire city can be blanketed by the gas."

"How does it affect humans and how do you avoid it?" Lynn asked now.

"Well it is an airborne virus, and it needs to be inhaled to take effect. Anyone one wearing the proper bio masks can survive, or if they are in an area, room or other place that is sealed off from the contaminated air when the gas is released. The gas and virus will dissipate after a few hours, the virus doesn't survive long after it is spread and subjected to oxygen. I'd say about two hours after initial release is when it becomes inert. I'd also say that the survival rate for a city this large would be about twenty percent."

"So we get gas masks for everyone in Vegas?" Weber spoke up.

"That would be impossible," the scientist said, not catching the irony.

Goodson said, "Well, we have twenty-three hours to pray for rain, or get our asses in gear and find Hulland.

I asked the scientist, "What would Hulland have to do to set off the reaction?"

"He could just pour the chemicals together in some kind of a container and they would do their work to form the cloud."

"Great, now we have to find a madman in a gas mask carrying Tupperware." I half-heartily joked.

**

Chapter 28

Trapper walked into the conference room and was nabbed by Weber standing next to the door. "I hate to say this but I'm sort of glad to see you. This place is like a funeral parlor, no humor; you make me smile even if you are a pain in the ass."

"Thank you Captain, I'll take that as a compliment." Trapper surveyed the room seeing us standing around a desk with computer monitors set up. He turned to Weber and said, "So, any word on Hulland?"

"None and we have twenty-three...," looking at his watch, "twenty-two hours before he lets the plague loose on the city. I've called my family and told them to leave the city, I didn't say why, but they are going to be quiet about it. You have any loved ones here to warn?"

Trapper thought about Sam and her brother. "Captain, I think you can handle this without me for a bit, but I'll be back." He turned and went out of the room. Weber came over to our group at the computer.

"Hulland has gotten the total bids up to the billions," Goodson said. "We decided to let the web feed go on, since he already has given us a time frame. Besides, this will allow us to see who our enemies are; this works out well for us. We are relaying this intel to Washington."

I had seen Trapper come in and then go out. I went to Weber, "Where's Trapper going?"

"I think he remembered someone to warn about getting out of the city. He said he'd be back," Weber replied.

"Have you made your peace with your maker?" I asked with a smile.

"My mother and father are my makers and they are both passed. I have a brother and I warned him already. Jim you have to do your magic and find this guy."

"I'll try but there's not much to go on at this point. Twenty-two hours isn't a lot of time to find one nut in a million people."

"Well, we can panic the public and arrest anyone who isn't running," Weber said with a big grin.

The computer tech was still trying to follow the wireless broadband signal but Hulland was on the move, every half hour a new place. He wasn't dumb. While we watched the computer, a uniform from Metro came up to Lynn and said something to her, she smiled and looked to me, "The men I sent to pick up the sheriff said he wasn't there. No body, no blood."

"Crafty old cop," I said quietly.

I took Penny and Buck out for a meal, we weren't getting anywhere at the moment and I was hungry. We went to a Subway and ate our food as we watched the city moving and shuffling to a beat that can only be heard if you listen carefully. We finished and went back to my car, driving over to Metro. I noticed there seemed to be a buildup of military vehicles in the lot. I saw a group of soldiers all lounging in the grassy area behind the parking lot; they were in combat uniforms and had packs on the ground by them along with rifles. I also saw the gas mask packs that I had to endure when I was in the Army. I figured that Goodson would get Vegas under military law eventually.

I sat in the car thinking about the chaos that would happen if the gas were released. Just the car accidents alone would create a mess causing people to panic worse and then when their breathing had increased from fear they would inhale the fumes, death would follow quickly.

Penny made me jump when she touched my arm and asked, "What were you being so far away about?"

"I was just imagining the devastation. Not something I should dwell on. Shall we go in and see if they have any news?"

They had no more than before we left; a couple sightings on Hulland amounted to Elvis sightings. Then one airman on a phone called over to Captain Goodman. "I got a person on the line who says they were suspicious of a van that was parked on his street. He thought it might be a predator near the children's playground. He came up to listen to what the man was saying in the back and said it sounded like he was on a cell phone talking about some attack on Vegas. The man doesn't know what it was about, but he's on his cell phone right now at the scene."

"Scramble a team to that location now! Tell the witness to get back, but keep on the line. This sounds like the set up Hulland would have, a mobile base and communications. If we move we may have him."

Lynn looked at the address the airman wrote and turned to Deacon and me, saying "Lets follow, it's better than sitting here." She gathered her things and told Williams to keep her informed on any changes by cell phone, he said he would.

I told Penny to wait here as Buck followed me out the door behind Lynn and Deacon. We got into Lynn's unmarked cruiser and she sped off in the direction of the address. I didn't see any military vehicles ahead or behind us. I hoped they were being dispatched from another location. We drove quickly out Tropicana and over to Jones Boulevard, down to a subdivision off the highway. We were coming down the street as we saw a swarm of Army Jeeps and Humvee's barreling down the street from the other end. They came to a screeching halt at the van parked on the side of the road, and jumped out with assault rifles at ready. We stayed back not wanting to be in the middle of a firestorm of bullets, if they got crazy.

One of the officers carefully went up to the van and did a cautious peek inside. He ran around the back as his men surrounded the vehicle and he pulled open the back doors. He stood looking in and then screamed to run! Everyone scattered just before the van blew up sky high. Luckily, no one was hurt, and the van was blazing now as the soldiers were trying to re-organize. I looked over to a home just across the street and saw someone watching between the houses behind some bushes. I slapped Lynn on the shoulder and pointed. "It's Hulland!"

Area 51 Murders

We jumped out of the car as Lynn was yelling to the soldiers and pointing. We ran as Hulland went around the building and was now running down the alleyway behind the house. We were in pursuit just as he went around a garage and before we got there Hulland had a car and was driving away. The owner of the car had left it running as he gathered some boxes from his porch to put in the car. We weren't going to be able to get back to our cars to pursue, but got the plate number from the owner and Lynn called in a BOLO.

Captain Goodson was not happy as we returned. The man never seemed to be happy.

One of the men on the phones called to Goodson and he went there. "Sir, I have the Hulland subject on the phone."

Goodson grabbed the phone and said, "You are a lunatic Hulland! You won't get away with this." He went silent, just listening, then hung up. He turned to us and said, "Hulland said he had enough people wanting his formula, and is not happy that we are getting too close to him, he's moved the attack up. At six o'clock today, in four hours.

~~*~~

Hulland drove out to McCarran Airport in another car he just stole; dumping the one he fled with from where he had to sacrifice his van. He saw the police coming up the street and the military coming the other way and knew he

194

couldn't drive out, so he slid out the side door of the van after setting the timer on the explosives in the van. He wasn't happy about it, but what could he do? He drove into the area of the airport where the business commercial hangers were, to rent a plane. He lost his own private plane in the desert outside of Vegas when he flew in with Fred and the kid. He knew they rented small aircraft here and was going to do so, but as he pulled around to the front of the buildings, he saw a number of military jeeps with large machine guns attached to the backs. There were soldiers walking around the tarmac and he realized that he wasn't going to be renting a plane today. He had to think on this.

He had to be high enough in the air to release the chemicals, and a plane was his means of attack. But the military had figured this out although it wasn't a stretch of the imagination. He tried to remember if there were any people he knew who had private aircraft that he could borrow from, or just take. It was his game now. He could think of none, so he had to form another idea.

He drove back out of the airport and thought about going up to North Vegas Airport, but he'd probably find the same problem. He sat on the side of the road along the south fence of the runways and had to think. He looked around and an idea struck him. He had a new plan.

**

Chapter 29

I was feeling very frustrated now, I had no idea about what to do to stop this. I was thinking about why I even cared so much. I guess it was just something in me that wanted to see justice and prevent bad from happening. I looked to Penny and Buck standing in the hallway of Metro and thought that as much as I give myself credit for, I wasn't going to stop Hulland. If the powers of the military and the cops couldn't, why did I think I could. I was starting to doubt myself.

I was also concerned for the safety of my loved ones and friends. I went to Lynn and said, "I'm starting to think it's a good idea to vacate the area and take a few days exploring Bullhead City."

She stood looking frustrated herself. "I'm going to have a car ready for Deacon and I to get the hell out of town when we get word that Hulland has released the virus. I'm terribly sorry for the people who will die, but there's just too many to save and I can't walk on water. Unless we get some clue as to where to find Hulland we are running out of time. One hour and I think the bastard may have won."

I studied her face and looked to Deacon; he had the strain showing also. "Well, I have to start getting organized to head out. You have my cell phone number, and don't be a hero; this is not a bullet you're dodging." I smiled and turned to the door and went out hoping I would see my friends again. I went to Buck and he said he called

Maria and told her to get in her car and drive south out of town towards Bullhead, he would call her to let her know where he was when we arrived. I ruffled Willy's head as he stuck it out of his purse, looking like he had no care in the world. Animals don't kill for pleasure or evil intentions, they did it out of survival. Too bad humans were so screwed up.

We went to our cars, got in and drove out. I thought about going by the house to gather some clothes but time was running out and I wasn't sure if Hulland would go ahead of schedule since he has already changed it once. I figured we could buy clothes to change into when we got there. Buck was following in his T-Bird down Vegas Boulevard as I took one last look at the casinos and hotels in my rear view mirror, when I saw it.

I had a terrible thought. If I was wrong, it could be fatal, but if I was right, it could stop Hulland. I pulled over into the parking lot of Fry's Electronics store and went back to Buck's car. I told him what I thought and he stood looking at what I was talking about. I told him I was going to see if I was right, I wouldn't feel bad if he got out of the city to go see Maria. Penny got out of the car and came to us.

I turned to her and said, "I don't want any argument and we don't have any time to discuss it, I want you to go with Buck, I have something to do and I don't know if I'm right. I may not have time to get out if I'm wrong, but I may stop Hulland."

She smiled and said, "We don't have time to argue is right, so let's go do what you think is right since we don't have time to think. I trust you with my life and I'm not leaving you."

I couldn't convince her, I knew she was stubborn, so I said for everyone to get in our cars and go. I drove back up the strip heading to the tallest structure west of the Mississippi, the Stratosphere! Almost a half mile in the air, a perfect substitute to release the virus without having a plane.

I was breaking the law by speeding and luckily, traffic was light. I ran stoplights and whizzed around cars nearly running a few off the Boulevard. I was making good time and hoping Hulland stuck to his schedule. I thought about calling Lynn but if I were wrong, I would put them at risk. I had a big decision to make; I decided to wait on calling. We sped into the valet parking and jumped out ignoring the boys who parked the cars and ran into the building. I hated to admit it but I didn't like the Stratosphere ever since I was almost pushed off the top of it and this is where Lacey tried to commit suicide and luckily failed. We ran for the elevators to go to the top and I was pounding on the walls wishing the thing would go faster. Penny was trying to calm me and I kissed her to say I was all right.

We arrived at the top; I figured he would go as high as he could. "Buck, go that direction and see what you can find, call me if you have the time and see him." Buck went off and I turned to Penny, pushed her to a chair in the lobby of the restaurant, and told her to stay. "I don't want you in the way if Hulland tries something." She smiled and said she'd wait for me here. I ran off towards the viewing platform overlooking the valley of Las Vegas that

I knew was there from the last time I was up here, but this time I wasn't thinking about my fear of heights.

I came to the glass doors of the platform still fearing the height that I could see beyond the railings, but went through after pulling my Glock and looked around. The platform was empty and then I saw the gate on the side of the protective fence going to the maintenance deck under the roller coaster ride that ran around the top of the building. The gate was open, so I went to it and looked out. I saw a coffee can sitting by the edge of the deck, I thought it would work for the mixture of the chemicals, but I didn't see Hulland.

I was ready to go out and grab the can but Hulland came around a wide beam in the structure and had a gun pointed at me, he gave me a wink and fired. I was hit in my shoulder and fell back to the deck just outside the gate; I was in shock from the bullet hitting my shoulder and couldn't move. I saw him go to the can, open the first two vials of the accelerant chemicals, and dump them in the can. He looked to me and yelled over the wind, "Ready to die Richards?" Then he put on a chemical mask to protect himself.

I lay on the ground; feeling blood coming from my shoulder, my Glock was lying about three feet from me. As Hulland pulled the specimen jar out of a bag at this feet, I heard someone to my right yell, "Hulland, don't even think about doing that!" I looked and saw Buck standing at the gate with his nickel-plated .38 on Hulland.

Area 51 Murders

Hulland turned his head and through the mask, I could see his eyes grow; he twisted the cap on the jar quickly and dumped the virus into the already fuming mixture. He dropped the jar to the ground and reached for his gun, but by this time Buck was repeatedly blasting him, forcing him to jerk and twist backward until he came to the edge of the platform. Buck put one more between his eyes and Hulland stumbled backwards off the platform and dropped down the near half-mile distance to the ground.

Buck came rushing to me, helping me up as I looked over to the now smoking mixture at the edge of the Stratosphere. I wasn't a religious person but at that moment I was thinking about Penny and Willy and wished for a miracle. I was wondering how long before Buck and I would die, when I smelled something funny. It reminded me of something in my recent past. I went to the jar on the floor, picked it up, holding it to my nose, and realized what it was! Buck came up beside me as I mumbled, "That idiot sheriff had pulled the same stunt I did, and he switched the powders."

Las Vegas was about to be covered in the smell of talcum powder.

Lynn and Deacon were standing watching the EMS take care of my shoulder. Luckily the bullet didn't do any damage and passed through without hitting anything major. Penny was sitting next to me on the gurney and watched them patch me up temporarily until we could get to the hospital. Captain Goodson came off the platform with his men carrying a large box that I presumed held the can of now inactive chemicals.

He came to me and said, "Richards, the country owes you and your big friend a debt of gratitude for putting this to an end, thank you." He turned and followed the troops out. "Do we get a medal?" I said to myself. I looked to Buck as he stood grinning and I winked to him.

He came over and said, "All in a day's work for the Richards Investigating firm. Now who do we bill this to?"

Lynn laughed aloud and said, "Don't look at me, talk to the mayor."

**

Chapter 30

Hulland's body was delivered to the morgue and the city went on as it had every day. People rushing around not knowing how close they came to extinction. Actually, Buck and I were too late to stop Hulland's attempt to release the chemicals, if the sheriff hadn't switched the jars of powder, the city and I would be dead by now.

Metro PD was back to normal, chasing criminals and eating donuts. Weber was delighted that everything came out well and had called Trapper to see if he wanted to do lunch sometime. I guess when coming that close to death, you make amends.

Area 51 Murders

Penny went back to her show that had run repeats until she returned. She was told by Goodson not to mention the failed attack on the city, to prevent any panic. I figured the government didn't want the fact that they were working with bio-chemicals to be spread around. I knew that the Groom Lake base officials would clamp down on the chemicals availability and the formula copy that Hulland had was recovered from the bag he had with him.

Everyone was happy now. I had spent the better part of the day in the hospital being patched up from the gunshot wound and Buck was back to running his guard service as usual. Maria had been stopped by Buck before she got to Bullhead City and returned to go sit with him in his office. Trapper was with me to help get me around for now; he wasn't pleased that he missed all of the excitement, but he felt better knowing it ended well. He and Sam were going to get her brother into a clinic in Denver for his, or her, surgery. Trapper said he'd be gone for about a week while he and Sam spent time in Denver.

He laughed as I was getting ready to leave the hospital, I asked what was so funny.

"I took Phil back to see Rancid Ricky to return the loan. I had my friend Josh with me for backup. We went into the dry cleaning business and we went back to Ricky's office without being invited. Josh requested that Ricky's goon leave the room, they reluctantly did. I told Ricky why we were there and he started about the interest on the loan, I told Phil and Josh to go out while I discussed the facts of life to Ricky. They went out and I got about as close to the foul smelling pig as I could stomach and pulled my gun placing it between his beady eyes. I told him if he didn't quit bellyaching about interest or anything else pertaining to Phil, I would visit him in the night and pull the trigger. I had to get away from him as I think he peed his pants. It was hard to tell over his body odor. We left pleased."

"Glad you worked that out well. So was Sam impressed with your detecting?"

"Oh, she showed me her approval all last night," he laughed.

Trapper dropped me off at my home and I rested until Penny came home with Willy and joined me sitting back by the pool. "Hey Sweetie, home finally?"

"Yep, I'm done with the hospital, they say I'll live. How was your day?"

"It was good, nothing to top the last week, you out in Area 51 and then back here chasing terrorists. Just a typical week for our little family."

She excused herself to go change clothes and go for a swim. She went into the house just as my cell phone rang. I looked at the caller ID and smiled. It was the sheriff.

"You could have told me you weren't going to give Hulland the real virus," I said as I answered. "You made a lot of people tense up to the end."

"I just wanted to have a little fun and not hurt anyone. Hulland wasn't very bright, he took the virus even though the color was still wrong. Did you get him?"

"Yep, he was a splatter on the pavement of the Stratosphere after Buck shot him a few times."

"Good, didn't like the guy anyways. He shot me without blinking an eye. Son of a bitch."

"Yeah, how did you pull that off?"

"I had a feeling he would get the drop on me so I wore my protective vest and went to see him. We made the swap and he shot me but I pretended to be dead. He didn't even take the bag of money, I guess he just wanted to get out with the virus. If he had come over to take the money, I was ready to shoot him, but he left."

"Thanks for thinking about humanity enough to switch the virus. What did you do with the jar I had?"

"Well, I went to a drug store and bought the same specimen jar and some talc and poured the talc in the jar and that's what I gave him. I buried the real virus out in the desert just north of Bullhead City. The only way it will be found is if the prairie dogs dig it up."

"Where are you at?"

"That's for me to know and everyone else to wonder. Sorry, but I will send you a Christmas card later this year. Just don't believe the postmark. I sent some of the money to Louise to take care of her and Mitch, maybe they can get out of that dead end life. Well, got to go, just wanted to touch base and say thanks for helping Louise and Mitch. They appreciated it."

"Glad I could help and if you're ever in town I have a guesthouse you can use."

He said thanks and hung up. Penny came out a few minutes later and I told her about the call.

"So he wasn't a real bad guy then?"

"Nope he took money from a bad guy for something that wouldn't hurt anyone. He's okay by me. I have a feeling he may be back up in Rachel with Louise and Mitchell but I'm not going try and to find out."

We relaxed around the back yard the rest of the afternoon. I had called Buck see if he was doing good and he was. He drove by around eight just after Lynn and Deacon came by to visit. We sat out back having a BBQ of some steaks I had hidden away for a good occasion, this was one.

I told Lynn about the sheriff and she said, "He really didn't do anything wrong other than tie you up, you can press charges, if you want." I said I wouldn't. "He didn't give Hulland the actual virus so no law was broken and I have no problem with him. But what did he do with the virus? Goodson was bugging me about that."

"It's buried way out in the desert never to be seen again," I said.

"Well I hope Goodson has no problem with it."

We had our meal and sat around talking until about eleven, when Lynn and Deacon left. Penny went in the house and Buck and I sat watching the stars. "I supposed you bragged to Maria about your exploits?"

"I told her as much as I could before she had to go to the Tropicana for her show. I did give you credit for figuring out where Hulland was going to do the deed."

"Thanks for that."

"I think I'm going to take Maria back up to Rachel and stay at that place again, it was a nice room and we'll go out to that place where you can see the base and watch for flying saucers. You think they'll remember us?"

"Sure, and you can say you were actually inside Area 51 now, and you can tell everyone we stopped world domination by terrorists. We'll never be able to top this."

"True."

We sat quietly looking up at all the very bright stars on the clear night just as we saw a light come over the hills behind my home. It wasn't bright but it seemed to just glow rather than being a spotlight. It hovered over the hill for a few minutes as we watched. From the distance I figured it was moving but looked like it was in the same spot. Then it moved towards us coming down the hill and out over my home. It was still very high up but it stopped over us and just floated. I had my mouth wide open as I craned my head back to watch it. Buck was making gurgling noises and then the thing just shot off over the valley at a speed that would have been excessively fast for any jet. I wondered if anyone in Vegas had seen it. I looked to Buck who was all wide eyed and still had his mouth wide open.

"No, I'm not saying that was an alien craft. There's a logical explanation for it," I spoke first.

"Jim, admit it, you just saw an alien saucer. What else could it be? And don't say it was swamp gas, there are no swamps out here."

"Maybe the Groom Lake base is testing a new stealth plane?"

Buck was sitting up now, "Man you just won't admit it will you. We were just visited for a close encounter of the third kind."

"I don't want any encounters, I'll watch them on TV but not up close." I stood to go into the house to call Penny when I saw the being standing by the backyard gate. Buck made a noise again when he saw it also. It had a big bulging head and large round eyes with no eyelids and it was wrapped in some metallic cloth. It just stood looking at us and I was feeling weak in the knees. I didn't know what to do, should we say hello or run like hell. I had seen too many creature movies to know we could be zapped into dust if we did the wrong thing. Buck came up beside me causing me to jump.

"Jim it's here," he whispered.

We were watching the thing start to glide to us when the metallic cloth caught on a corner of the cement curb that went around the landscaping and it started to pull off the creature. The cloth dropped to the ground and I realized the creature was wearing a bikini and had boobs.

Damn! It pulled off the mask and there stood Penny laughing.

"Real funny Penny, but I knew it was you," I defended.

"Like hell, you should have seen your faces."

"Hey, did you see the light that just went over the house, it looked like a flying saucer," Buck asked.

"I saw no light, but I was wearing this mask. I'm going in for the night to relax, you macho men can sit out here and watch for aliens." She turned and went in. I looked to Buck, he wasn't smiling, we followed Penny inside and locked the doors.

All was quiet in the back yard as the light came over the house again and hovered before shooting straight up into the sky and disappeared.

THE END

For every ending there's a new beginning.

Bob Moats

Read a preview of the next book, "Mortuary Murders."

Chapter 1

The funeral home was crowded with well-wishers. Abundant flowers surrounding the coffin gave the viewing room a sickly mixture of fragrances, as Penny sat on a chair while people huddled around her, expressing their condolences.

Buck was standing before the coffin looking down at the body of Jim Richards, looking like he was made of wax. He probably was, since the explosion of Jim's Crown Vic had thrown his body from the car, most of his face was damaged and Buck thought that the funeral people did a good job of filling in the missing pieces around his face. Buck couldn't believe his friend was gone. He turned away and went to sit next to Penny as she held up well for her loss.

The director of the home closed the coffin and the guests were allowed to take a little time to talk about the recently departed. Lynn and Deacon talked about the cases he helped the police with around Las Vegas, Trapper talked about how Jim and he first met, over murder of course. I suddenly realized I was in an enclosed place; I was claustrophobic and started to scream for help. The coffin suppressed my screams, no one heard me as they lowered the coffin into the ground.

I was still screaming while Penny was shaking me in our bed. Damn, I hated realistic dreams like that. I sat up in the bed as Penny stood next to me now; I was sweating profusely and shaking.

"What the hell were you dreaming about? That was worse than the time you dreamt you were going down on the cruise ship."

"Crap, it was worse. You know I'm claustrophobic, I was dreaming I was in my coffin, but still alive. Damn dreams anyway. You were there, mourning me and Buck was there along with our friends. After they closed the coffin, I guess I woke and found I was in the dark and in a closed box. I was screaming, but no one could hear me because of the coffin."

"A coffin? That's not good Jim, it's bad juu-juu to dream about a coffin."

"Bad juu-juu? Have you gone voodoo now? You know I just got back from being out in Area 51 and had to go to a funeral home to help take Mark Huston's body in. I was all over the funeral home including the embalming room where ME Joe Lang did the autopsy on Mark. I guess my mind put that experience together with me in the coffin. Not a good thing, okay, bad juu-juu."

Penny was laughing so I slapped her on the butt, causing her to jump on me and she made good juu-juu to me.

We went out to the kitchen about a half hour later and I did my morning toast ritual. The new toaster that we bought last month worked very well, I was happy with it. Penny made her oatmeal and I sat at the snack bar with my toast as our toy Yorkie, Willy, was eyeing my food. I broke off a piece and dropped it to him on the ground.

"So what do you have planned for today?" she asked me.

"I haven't the foggiest idea. I'm going into the office and just sit until someone comes in to hire me to solve their mystery. I'm not taking any cases about aliens or going to Area 51 again. One time was enough for me."

"Well, you can sit thinking about how you saved Las Vegas from total annihilation at the hands of a terrorist."

"The military said to keep that on a low key, but I guess I can revel in my thoughts."

Penny went out to get ready for work just as my cell phone rang and the caller ID said it was Deacon. "Hey, big guy, what's up?"

"I need you to settle a debate I'm having with Klein over in missing persons. If a body from a funeral home turns up missing does it go to missing persons, homicide or to robbery?"

I felt a very cold chill run up my spine; the dream crept back into my head at the mention of a body from a funeral home. Coincidence?

"Was the man murdered?" I asked hesitantly.

"No," Deacon said quickly.

"Well, that lets you out. The guy isn't alive so he's not a person, therefore he is a property now and his body was robbed from the funeral home. So I'd say Robbery Division should handle it."

"That's what I said, but everyone is passing the buck. Actually, the body wasn't stolen from a funeral home, he was taken from a mortuary that preps bodies for burial. A business I could never do."

"What did Lynn say about the buck passing?"

"She's not here; she's in LA to testify on a homicide we closed a year ago, it's coming to trial now. The machines of justice turn slowly."

"Well, keep me informed about your missing body. On second thought I don't want to know, it's grim to think someone would steal a body."

"Or he turned into a zombie and walked out," Deacon said with a laugh.

"Then you'd better hide. I'm going into my office to sulk and wait for crime to come to me. If you get bored you can stop by to visit."

"I'll think about it. Anything to get away from here before Weber finds me by myself. Talk later." He hung up and I put my phone back in my pocket and waited for Penny to go to work. If you can call it work, she sits and talks to people in front of TV cameras and has women do her hair and make-up. Four hours of sitting around, an easy life.

She came out, gathered her purse and briefcase, gave me a kiss on the nose, and said, "I may stop in to see you when I get done for the day. We can do lunch at Bistros."

"That's sounds good to me, be careful driving in." I didn't want to mention Deacon's call about the missing body from the mortuary so soon after my dream, she likes to put things together to make a big deal out of it.

After she left, I gathered my equipment to go to the office. I put Willy in his travel bag as I was calling it now, I didn't think it was appropriate for me to carry a purse. We went out to the garage, got the Crown Vic out and drove over to my building. I waved to the guard at the back parking lot gate and put the car into my reserved space.

I entered the building, let Willy loose and went by Trapper's office, he wasn't in. I stopped at Buck's door, he wasn't in. I was wondering if anyone was working today. In the lobby I found Lacey busy reading a woman's magazine.

"We have no work to do today?"

She about jumped out of her skin when she heard me, I had that effect on her. She calmed herself and said, "No, it's boring so far. Trapper took Sam and her brother to Denver for his surgery yesterday and Buck is home sleeping because he had to fill in for a guard last night at the new dealership."

"So it's just you, Willy and me today, huh?"

"Afraid so, unless someone comes in."

213

Area 51 Murders

"Well, anyone wanting me to chase aliens, send them away," I said and went to my private office.

I spent the morning exploring the internet on my computer finding information about dreams, coming up with a bunch of mumbo-jumbo, and finally closed the internet down. I sat back staring at the poster I had made of Penny in her bikini from a picture I took on our mystery cruise. She didn't mind that I put it on my wall, she looked good in it.

I heard the front door bell tinkle and waited to see what was going on. Lacey came to my door and said, "You are needed."

I got up, went out, and found a very somber looking man in a black Brooks Brother's suit that must have cost him a week's salary. He was very straight-laced looking, pencil mustache, and his hair was slicked back, reminding me of a gangster from the old black and white movies. Adolphe Menjou, the "suave" and "debonair" star of Hollywood movies from the 20's to the 40's came to mind. He had that bearing.

"Hello, I'm Jim Richards, may I help you?"

"I hope so; the police officer who called about my missing body said you were the man for the job. His name was DeAngelo" he said clearly and with great pronunciation.

"Yes, Detective DeAngelo, we're friends. Please come to my office." As we went, I realized what he had said, about a missing body. I was getting chills again and asked him to sit when we entered the room.

"And you are?"

"I'm Thomas Hannigan. Mr. Richards, I hope you can be discreet about my problem, it looks bad for business to have a body come up missing."

"Just what is your business exactly?" I asked.

"I'm a mortician; I prep bodies for funeral homes and save them the trouble and expense of maintaining a mortuary in their funeral homes. It works well for me, but to have a body come up missing, this is not good for business."

"So you want me to find the body. Can't the police help you on that?"

"There would be inquiries and police snooping around my establishment. Besides the police can't figure who to send to handle the case, I told Officer DeAngelo to forget it, I would handle it myself. That's when he recommended you."

"It's Detective DeAngelo and I'll have to personally thank him."

Yeah, with a shot to the head.

**

Continued in the book...

Area 51 Murders

~~*~~

Jim Richards Family of Readers

Thanks to the following people who are now part of the Jim Richards Family of Readers. They have read a book or more and enjoyed them. They all volunteered to be included in the list. If you are a fan of the books, send me your full name and you will be included in future books. Send your name to murdernovels@bobmoats.com to be added here and on the website.

* Achim Feifel * Al Norris * Alex Wheatley * Alexandra Delporte-Wilkinson * Amy Tapia * Andrea Bryan * Anne Shepherd * Arianda Sugar * Arlene Markowski * Ashley Augustus * Audra Hall * Barbara Hughes * Barbara Sammons * Barbara Schuler * Barbara Zirger * Beth Donohue Plenskofski * Betsy Childress * Beth Gibson * Bill Sandy * Bill Tornquist * Billie-jo Collie * Boni J Rychener * Carl Bishopric * Carla Lewis * Carole Henderson * Carolyn Conroy * Carolyn Riddle-Linington * Cassy Bailey * Cathie Turner * Chad Hudson * Charlotte L Duran * Cheryl L. Everett * Cindy Ackley Nunn * Cindy Valstad * Connie Bancroft * Corinne Kay O'Daniel * Dana Robbins Chuchran * Dana Wichita * Danielle Monique * Darren Heald * Dave Travers * David Wilkinson * DeAnn Jannereth * Deanna Miller * Deb Breuker Balbo * Debbie Carter * Debbie White * Deborah

Bob Moats

Fartuch * Deborah Gauze * Deborah Sullivan * Dee King * Denise Freeman * Diana Carver * Dixie Beck * Donna Gould * Donna Thompson * Donny Minter * Doris Kight * Eddie Moore * Eric Walters * Felicia Annette Bradfield * Francine Menor * Gail Chesney * Georgiann Minster * George Conner * Greg Colucci * Hayley Rankin * Harold Garcia * Heidi Arnold * Irma Ranee Coy * Jacqueline Moss * Jan Kimball * Janice Schneider * Janice Spoor * Jennifer Redmond * Jessica Keown-Belous * Jim Beck * Jo Boguslaw * Jo Turner * Joanne Marie Turner * John Peiffer * John Wisbiski * Joseph Wauro * Joyce Stacy * Joyce Trifiletti * Judy Franklin * Judy Travers * Judy Padgett * Julie Heath * Junnahvee Benson * Karen Dahl * Karen Grams * Karen Higham * Karen Kaiser * Karen Meinburg Richwine * Karen Kirkman Parker * Karin Hawkins * Karin Vasvari * Kathleen Donohue Roesing * Kathleen Riddle-Wolfe * Kathy Hinds Moore * Kathy Jones * Kathy Mitchell * Katie Benzler * Kay Burns * Kelly Garcia * Ken Boggs * Keota Rodriguez * Kiera Mccarthy * Kim Estes * Kitty Stolle * Kristie Sciler * Kirsty Stanton * LaLonnie Scallen * Larry Morris * Leann Parr * Lenora Scales * Leslie Marie Jackson * Linda Forester * Linda Ingle Cox * Linda Kennerö * Linda Magill * Lisa Bower * Liz Gibson * Lorraine Wiman * Loretta Alexander * Lynda Bowles * Lynette Lawrance * LuAnn Louttit * Manny Rothman * Marcia Gibson DeWitt * Marie Calder * Marlene Bryan * MaryLouise Kramp * Mary Lynn Gross * Megan Atkins * Meghan Hyden * Melody Cannavan * Michael Carruthers * Michael Dinkens * Michael Vannoy * Michelle Burns-Mitchell * Michelle Pilcher * Micki Potter * Mike Moats * Mimi Baur * Myrna Hecht * Nadine Sutton * Nancy Ellen Sayre * Natalie Quine * Neena Martin * O'Della Wilson * Pat Pollington * Pat Rohn * Patricia Jarmon * Patricia C Trezza * Patrick Barry * Paul Lawrance *

Area 51 Murders

Peggy Davis * Phyllis Bassett * Raylene Matheny * Rebecca Collins Besner * Renee Brumley * Reta Hanna * Reta Moats * Roberta Navarro-Harder * Sally Berneathy * Sally Hubler * Sarah Santos * Satka Nikc * Sharon E. Edwards * Sharon Mangini * Sharon McMillon * Sheena Rawl * Sherry Amstutz * Shirley Alvarez * Shirley Davies * Shirley Williams * Stacie Rowe * Stephanie Conner * Steve Cullen * Susan Haughton * Susan Hesse Adams * Susan Salomon * Suzan K Chase * Taisha Cullum * Tamara Moore * Tammy Castleberry * Tammy Lynn Wood * Ted Murphy * Terri Atkins * Terri Creech * Terry Raab * Tonia Rachael Riggs-Williams * Travis Fleury-Lopez * Twyla Gawlas * Val Brooks * Walt Munsel * Yvonne Isakson *

Thank you to all these wonderful people.

Thank you for purchasing this book. I hope you enjoy it as much as I enjoyed writing it for my faithful readers. Please feel free to email me to tell me what you thought about my stories. I love hearing from the readers. I can be reached at murdernovels@bobmoats.com thanks again!